First published in the United States of America by

HiDef Media Group

2700 Executive Park Drive

Cleveland, Tennessee 37312

Telephone: (423) 339-8717

Fax: (423) 476-7166

www.hidefmg.com

ISBN 978-1-932496-68-0

Cover photo by: Alana Goldstein

Art direction by: HiDef Media Group

Cover design by: Heather Rogers, HiDef Media Group

Interior layout by: www.delaney-designs.com

Dedicated to

Cincinnati Children's Hospital Medical Center

Foreword

by Thomas H. Inge, MD, PhD

We are in the midst of an obesity epidemic the likes of which the world has never seen. In the U.S., more than two thirds of adults are obese or overweight, while about a third of all children suffer with a weight problem. What is fascinating though is that we see nearly the same proportion (about 5%) of adults and kids experiencing extreme obesity. For that extremely obese group, the adverse social and medical impacts of the disease are far more poignantly felt. In *The Fat Boy Chronicles*, Lang Buchanan takes the reader vividly into the day-to-day life of an extremely obese teenager who chooses to fight back against the all-too-common abuse, defeat, sadness, neglect, and ridicule facing kids with a weight problem. The extraordinary aspect of this story is how we (and the teen) arrive at a certain peaceful calm after a raging battle. Set in Cincinnati, Ohio, the authors demonstrate the magnitude and power of the social stigmatism, isolation, peer confrontation, and inner conflict experienced by millions of American teens of today who are just like Jimmy Winterpock.

How did it come to this? This is a tough one. First, we are what we eat. But it is obviously more complicated. In reality, what is most important is both the quantity and quality of the calories that we eat, and the number that we burn in physical activity every day. But the deck is clearly stacked against us and our kids. The deck is also stacked more against Blacks and Hispanics. We started out this human existence with a version of our genes assembled at a time when food was far less plentiful, but was actually healthier: it was never processed nor stuffed full of artificial sweeteners and flavorings. And in those ancient times, our genes and our metabolism were more efficient because we also had to work a lot harder to survive. Fast forward to now. Most people regularly praise the modern conveniences that allow us to lead faster-paced lives and eat on the run. We seldom dwell on the fact that the processing that makes frozen foods possible strips healthy ingredients, like vitamins and fiber, from vegetables. And, who complains about it when we get larger than necessary portion sizes? For sure, we don't pay much attention to the inundation in our diet, especially drinks targeted to kids, of high fructose syrup. HFS is the key ingredient that many scientists, including Rob Lustig at UCSF, feel is a major contributor to the obesity problem. HFS is a toxin causing fatty liver disease seen in adults and kids alike. Besides a diet of toxic food, we're also not getting the physical workouts our ancestors took for granted. We spend hours passively watching television and playing video games; we take the elevator instead of the stairs.

Extreme obesity is disease....a disease that affects kids and adults in ways we are only now starting to unravel. For instance, obese kids have a quality of life that is on par with kids stricken with cancer. Kids that are extremely obese actually report that the quality of their day-to-day life is actually much worse than those with cancer! This is in part due to the merciless teasing and cruelty of other kids. And, it is in part because these kids have aches and pains similar to those that 50 and 60 year olds have; it is astonishing how an extra 75-100 pounds of weight early in life can place wear and tear on the joints decades ahead of what is expected. It is in part because these kids are denied the simple pleasures and necessities in life that we all want to enjoy: amusement park rides, long walks on the beach, and even the safety and peace of mind that a seat belt offers to passengers. But beyond this, obesity can adversely affect most organ systems in the human body. It contributes to diabetes, breathing and sleep disorders, high blood pressure, high cholesterol, heart disease, asthma, skeletal deformities, depression, dementia later in life, and major disruptions in fertility just to name a few.

Obesity shares another similarity with cancer. Both can be difficult if not impossible to reverse. We often say that obesity must be prevented, since treatment options have seldom been successful. Indeed, most of us can lose a few pounds of weight, but recognize that the vast majority of us then put that weight back on plus some. And what about the kid who is about 100 pounds overweight? We see this level of obesity in about 2% of kids in grades 5-12 in the Greater Cincinnati area. We also see that over a 5 year period only 1 in 10 can reduce weight enough to shed the title "extremely obese." Sadly, you also find that on average, these same kids gain 1 inch on their waistline every year. In fact, most kids in this extreme category of obesity already harbor 2 or more risk factors for cardiovascular disease. By the time they become adults, there is a 100% chance they will remain obese, and they can look forward to loss of 10-20 years of life due to their weight problems. Big kids face big health problems.

The two main components to any successful weight loss program are diet and exercise; however, depending on the amount of excess weight, usual efforts may not be enough to get to a normal healthy weight. Our bodies give priority to energy (fat) stores since long ago these stores were very important to individual survival and reproductive capacity. So we find that each of our cells has hung onto those very genes that promote energy intake and storage and that minimize energy expenditure, as if our own bodies were designed to fail us when we try to shed weight. In fact, many scientists, like Rudy Leibel at Columbia University, have published examples of how our subconscious mind and core metabolic processes strongly defend our body weight against the attack of a "diet," even when we really need to lose weight. Metabolism will slow and physical activity will subconsciously decrease during dieting in an effort to oppose the weight loss attempt!

So what message does this send? Are the problems so complex and the solutions so elusive that there is no hope? I don't think so. Back to basics for a moment: prevention of weight gain is always the first focus.

Learning about and advocating for more opportunities for kids to get physical activity is clearly a goal. Getting greater access to healthy foods and learning and practicing how to avoid unhealthy foods is also possible. We also need to figure out ways to systematically ignore the misinformation about nutrition that advertisers want to share with us and our kids, and learn nutrition facts from someone who cares about our health and is not just trying to sell us something.

Due to the complex nature of obesity we should not be surprised that there is not a clear one-size-fits-all answer to reverse it. For those suffering with obesity, weight loss is a challenge, but the battle is winnable. Just ask Jimmy Winterpock. While his solution may or may not be the answer for others, motivation for change is paramount. What is known is that it takes time, education, a lot of effort, and teamwork by the family. Sometimes it takes the advice of doctors to help with the medical and physiological complexities. And for years to come, it will take advocacy, a voice in government, and greater research efforts to overcome the weight and health problems facing a large proportion of our nation. The good news is that these efforts may be working—at least for some groups. According to a 2008 report from the Centers for Disease Control, there may finally be an improvement in rates of obesity in Whites in the U.S. Even so, that is still not enough. We want to see reversal of obesity numbers for all races and ethnic groups of kids and adults alike before declaring that the problem is turning around. We need to keep the pressure and advocacy on point. In this regard, thanks to both Jimmy and Lang Buchanan.

Thomas H. Inge, MD, PhD
Director of the Comprehensive Weight Management Program
Director of the Teen Longitude Assessment of Bariatric Surgery
Associate Professor
University of Cincinnati College of Medicine
Cincinnati Children's Hospital Medical Center
www.cincinnatichildrens.org/weight

the fat boy chronicles

INSPIRED BY A TRUE STORY

DIANE LANG
MICHAEL BUCHANAN

A TIN ROOF FILMS NOVEL

HiDEF
MEDIA GROUP

Tuesday, 8-15

Hey, Mrs. Pope. I'm the diet-challenged kid who sits in the last seat by the door. I'm probably bigger now than I was this morning because your class is right after lunch and homeroom. I stay in the back so you don't have to constantly hear, "We can't see around Jimmy!" Just trying to help out. Besides, you can see a lot back here in the cheap seats. Like how nobody wants to do this stupid journal.

Man, I don't get teachers. Why do you guys pile it on the first day of school? Can't you let us get used to the idea that summer is really over, before you stick it to us? Man, this journal thing has me bummed, big time. Three half-pages a week is tough. That's so NOT cool. It may not seem like much to you (Hello! You're an English teacher), but for kids like me, it stinks. That's almost two pages every week for an entire school year. Why don't you just ask us to write the great American novel and say it's due in June? It's not as bad for the girls. They keep diaries and write notes to each other nonstop. They write really big, too. Just to take up space. That's so fake.

Like any of us are going to write more than three times a week. Half the kids won't even do that. It's too much to expect from us. I don't have that much to write about anyway.

No offense, but some of the topics you suggested are cheesy, like "describe your room." My room has four walls, a bed and a dresser. I have a built-in desk with a lamp. Last week my mother and I pasted glow-in-the-dark stars on my ceiling. Okay, that's pretty cool. But now what do I write about?

English teachers should have their students write essays

about current events like we did last year in middle school, not just any stuff you want to write about. What's the point of that? There's enough garbage in the world already.

You said to write really fast even if it makes no sense, so here I am writing a journal that makes no sense, or is that nonsense, or maybe nose sense, or stupid sense, or, in my pocket are no cents, or the locker room has lots of scents. So, I'm done. There's my OVER a half-page. Sorry this is stupid, but what do you expect from a high school kid? Hope you enjoyed me ruining a tree.

Wednesday, 8-15

If you really are reading this, I'm surprised. My English teacher two years ago made us keep a journal and she never read them. We got check marks and either "that's nice" or "good work" comments. I could've written that I was a space alien and she would've put, "That's nice." She collected everyone's journal at the same time though. Your way is better— a different row every week. That way you might have time to actually read them.

You said that if we didn't want you to read something in here, we should fold it and label it Please Don't Read This Page. How do we know you really won't read it? What if we don't feel like writing three journals a week, and just write the same thing over and over again? You really couldn't do anything about it, because if we marked two of them Please Don't Read This Page, you couldn't admit that you really read them, or the class would think you were a scammer. And if you don't make comments unless we ask you to, what's the point of writing a journal? You're supposed to give us feedback about our writing. I don't get your whole thing about "freeing our writing muse" (I didn't know my muse was locked up) and "oiling our inner tin man." Some people might think you're really weird. Not me though. Ever since my mom made me watch *The Dead Poet's Society*, I've kinda expected English teachers to be "out there."

But I'm not sure how we're going to "free our muse" if we think our English teacher might read our stuff. Like we're going to write anything bad. I'm not the sort of kid who gets into trouble or uses bad language, so I don't have anything to worry about anyway. But what if I was a smoker or doing drugs or something? Or had girlfriends? Like I would write about all that in here. Besides, a kid like me having a girlfriend? Yeah, right.

I think your class will be okay. I'm excited about high school and learning things. I don't play sports. I would like to be on a team but can't right now because of my weight. And contact lenses would help. Last time I tried out for club soccer, I kept losing my glasses. It was a real pain.

We moved here over the summer, so I don't have many friends yet. It's bad enough being a freshman and getting picked on all the time by the older kids, but it's worse when you don't have anyone to share the grief with.

If you really are reading this, I have a request. Can you move Ricky Stockton away from me? He smells really bad.

Friday, 8-18

Hanover High's a lot bigger than Adams Middle. It takes forever to get from the math hall to the foreign language hall. And we only have five minutes between classes, which sucks. It's too far to go to my locker and if I do, I have a hard time getting to class on time. Yesterday, I went to the wrong class during 3rd period. I sat in social studies for like ten minutes before I realized I was in the right room, but I was an hour early. I got my schedule all mixed up and I was supposed to be in Spanish. My teacher didn't realize until he called roll. It was embarrassing to walk out while everybody laughed.

At lunch, we have to eat so fast, by the time I get there and get my tray, I've only got a few minutes left. I mean, this isn't an eating contest at the county fair, where you stuff as many hot dogs and pies in your face as you can. Actually, that sounds pretty good right now, cause I'm hungry.

I haven't found many people to sit with yet. Just a few kids, mostly girls, from my youth group. It's hard being in a new school where you don't know hardly any guys, except this one kid from my old school, but he's a real jerk.

Your class is okay but algebra really inhales, if you know what I mean. The teacher writes on the overhead all period and then gives us worksheets. I can hardly stay awake. If it wasn't for Scott, the kid who sits next to me, I would go to sleep. He has "stomach problems" and it keeps us up. When Mr. L walked by, he coughed and looked straight at me. I put my hands up and shook my head and said I didn't do it. Mr. L smirked and went back to his projector.

Monday, 8-21

School really sucks. I hate it here. Middle school was bad, but at least people talked to me. Sometimes.

Tuesday, 8-22

On the bus ride home today, I sat with a kid named Allen. He's overweight, but in a worse way than me. I mean, he's not any bigger than me, he just doesn't get it. Like, he wears these big pants that hang too far down, and you can see his underwear and sometimes a little more. The girls think it's gross and scream whenever his pants creep down too much. And his shirts are too short and half his gut hangs out. Sometimes, he really asks for all the grief he gets. Then he smiles all the time and tries to talk to people. Everyone ignores him, and I tried to, but got caught sitting with him in the front of the bus, which was a big mistake because we got bombed with paper wads. Then someone yelled for the bus driver to split us up—they said we were making the bus lean to one side. The driver hollered at everyone for messing up her bus, then made Allen and me pick up all the paper at our feet. Allen was huffing and puffing the whole time, and when we sat back down his face was really red. Of course, the rest of the bus cracked up laughing. Ha, ha. Real funny.

Now, I'm sitting in my room writing this journal. I still think it's a waste of time. I mean, who cares about my boring life? Hold on a minute. I don't believe it. My pimple-faced sister is yelling at me because she thinks I went in her room and snooped on her laptop. Jessica thinks she's cool because she's two years older than me.

Okay. She's finally gone. She gets hysterical over nothing. I mean, what if I did get on her laptop? She must have something big time to hide. It's like she's making me want to get into her computer. I don't have anything to hide on my laptop. I don't get that many e-mails and none of my friends do the online chat stuff.

She really scared Nanook, our dog. He's supposed to be the family dog, but he likes hanging out with me the most. He's a mutt, but he has a lot of sheepdog in him. When I'm playing my PS3, he likes to watch.

Thursday, 8-24

The teachers really pile on the homework in high school. My sister complained about it all the time last year; now I know why. Every teacher thinks their class is the only one. Not you. I like reading the short stories you've assigned so far. After reading the one about Doodle, I told my parents we should go to Florida to see a real ibis. My dad wanted to know why, so I told him about "The Scarlet Ibis." He thought I should talk about it in youth group. I might but church is not supposed to be like school. No offense, but I don't want to sound like an English teacher or anything, even though English is my favorite subject. (I'm not saying that just to suck up.)

My dad said there's so much pressure on kids today, it would be good to talk about some of the things in the story. I mean, look at Doodle. He died because his brother was ashamed of him and wanted him to be like everybody else. That's sad because most kids will do anything to fit in, like smoking or stealing things from people's garages. A lot of kids do worse things, like get into drinking and drugs. I tried chewing tobacco once, and hated it. I got so sick I turned green. My sister caught me and a friend from my old neighborhood chewing it and told on us. Boy, were my parents MAD. When I threw up in the front yard, my sister laughed at me. She can be a real jerk.

My parents talk to me about peer pressure all the time, but they really don't have to worry because I definitely do not fit in. Besides, there can't be pressure if there's not any peers. Maybe Doodle's parents should have spent more time with him, but they were probably embarrassed by him too. After all, they had a coffin made for him right after he was born—that's so NOT cool. If your own family's not on your side, how does a kid have a chance at anything?

Sunday, 8-27

Last night I finished my HW early and played against my dad on the PS3. He thought he could beat me. It sets off a spark inside of me, hearing him say this, because I refuse to lose to a person who was born thirty years before video games were even invented. I've been playing since the age of four and know for certain I can always beat him. And, I did.

Then, when I was watching a show on *Animal Planet*, my friend Paul called. He goes to Northview, but he's in my youth group at church. He was all weirded out because a body was found in the woods behind his house—he and his dad watched the police carry it out. Even though there was a white sheet over the stretcher, Paul said the body appeared all lumpy under the sheet. Like they couldn't lay it out straight. Like it had been in the woods for a long time.

It's creepy to think that a murderer dumped his victim a few hundred yards away from Paul's bedroom. I mean, the killer could've walked right by his window. Paul said his dad's been in a worse mood than usual because of it, and his mom's been screaming constantly. His parents aren't exactly what you'd call good examples, but Paul's real cool. He thinks the dead person is from Michigan or something, and the killer drove for hours until he found a safe neighborhood to hide the body. There aren't many murders in Hanover. In fact, until today, there weren't any. Man, I can't stop thinking about it. I hope I can fall asleep.

Monday, 8-28

I woke up this morning thinking about the dead body. Like, it's not even a person yet. Just an "it." The whole thing really freaks me out. It could be a kid or a grandpa—Paul thinks it's probably some girl, since most bodies found in the woods are female. It finally made the news; I watched it this morning while I was eating Pop-Tarts.

Man, the weekend went by way too fast. Last week was the longest and shortest week of my life. I felt like I was trapped going to school all week, but now it's over. This schedule is too fast-paced for me. There are so many things to keep up with— go to my locker, get my books, hurry to class, take notes, and repeat the whole thing like seven times a day.

Today was really hot, and it was even more disgusting than usual in the cafeteria. I don't think the air conditioning is working in there. Allen eats lunch when I do, so I finally have someone to sit with. Not that sitting with Allen is the greatest. He stuffs food in his mouth as fast as he can, like he's starving, and the other kids watch. Everything he brings for lunch really smells. I mean, why can't he pack something normal like peanut butter and jelly sandwiches? No, he has to bring tuna fish, salami, sausage, and rotten cheese. One day he even brought sardine sandwiches. That's so not cool. I half expect him to bring pig's feet or sheep brains. It wouldn't surprise me one bit. Then he talks with his mouth open and it's pretty disgusting. I try not to watch him, but he sits right in front of me.

When he's not stuffing his face, he's okay and is into some really cool hobbies, like chess, Warcraft, and he has some serious Yu-gi-oh cards with heavy hit point potential. (Not that he's trading.) He's an online warrior like me. He's actually kind of a legend in the gaming world. His online handle is KillingMachine and the dude earned it. I've seen him play and he is absolutely ruthless. I always imagined him to be some pumped-up Arnold the Terminator kind of guy. It just goes to show how much you can hide on the Internet. I wonder if any of the other kids at school know exactly who's kicking their butts.

Thursday, 8-31

Mom's making my lunch everyday now, since I told her about not having much time to eat. She fixed two PBJ's this morning, and I stuck them in my backpack. I forgot they were there and put books on top of them. (I usually carry my lunch separately, but lately some kids on the bus have threatened to take it). The sandwiches were squished as thin as a CD and the sticky grape jelly leaked through the paper sack and got all over my math book. At lunch, when I remembered I had sandwiches, I pulled them out and had to peel them off the bag. At least I provided entertainment for Allen.

Allen and I talked some about the murder. He thought it was awesome that it happened practically in Paul's backyard. Guess that makes Paul almost a celebrity. Paul says the police are all over the crime scene still, like 24/7. And, he said there's been lots of news trucks in his neighborhood, some parked in front of his house.

I hate having math second period; it's all I can do to stay awake in there. Then today, in the middle of a really boring class, Mr. L gave us a riddle about sheep. He asked, "If a farmer had 26 sheep and one died, how many would he have left?" Almost all the class said 25, except for Scott, trying to be funny, replied "420." Mr. L claimed that we were all wrong. I guess old men get pleasure from riddles that make about as much sense as a Popsicle stick joke. It drives me nuts.

We also got our gym outfits in PE today. That means we'll have to start dressing out soon. I wish I didn't have to take PE.

Saturday, 9-2

It's been all over the news—the dead body found behind Paul's house. Just in time for Labor Day weekend. Kind of takes away from the whole family picnic scene. No one around here feels like celebrating much.

In case you missed it, the victim was a seventeen-year-old girl from Wilmington High named Kimberly Taylor. We play them in football and they usually beat us. Wilmington is a nice, safe place like Hanover. Well, it used to be.

My mom read about the murder in the *Cincinnati Enquirer* today. Under the cause of death it said, "Homicidal violence, type undetermined." The police said Kimberly was wearing a Danskin hooded sweatshirt over a medium-top with sequins. She had a nose stud with a clear stone and a silver ring on her finger. Her boyfriend is the prime suspect. Paul thinks we should hide in the woods to see if anyone shows up. He read somewhere that the killer always returns to the scene of the crime.

Monday, 9-4

Please Don't Read This Page

Yesterday was the first day of dressing out in PE. I hoped it would be different here but I guess I was wrong. We wear a red shirt with Patriot PE on the front and shorts to match. I tried to find a locker over in the corner so I could change shirts without anybody noticing me. I didn't realize that the football players use the corner I picked. I was already there when several came in, talking and cutting up. By the time I got my shirt and t-shirt off, I could tell they were looking at me. My neck turned hot with embarrassment and I faced away from them so they couldn't see my chest. One of the guys said, "Hey, aren't you in the wrong locker room? People with tits like that should be on the other side." I didn't turn around or answer him. I pulled my PE shirt down and crammed my things in my locker. I half ran through the benches, trying to get out of there as fast as I could. Just as I was pushing open the door to the gym, I heard Robb Thuman, the star quarterback, say, "Maybe our mascot should be the Tomatoes instead of the Patriots.

We've got one right here." Everyone was laughing. When I went in the gym, I sat on the bottom row so I wouldn't have to climb the steps. Coach Bronner called roll. I raised my hand when he called my name and he looked at me over his glasses. "You don't have to raise your hand, son. Just say 'here.'" I said, "Yes, sir," but he kept looking at me. In the stands behind me, Robb said, "Just say, 'Tomato, present and accounted for.'" Coach cut his eyes up there but said nothing to him.

When we got dressed after class, I waited till everyone was gone before I changed. They were all out in the hall ready to leave while I sat in the locker room. It really hurts to have someone say those things. Don't they know that I try to be a good person, and that I would cheer for them at the football games? Like I wouldn't want to be on the team, running all over and not sweating like crazy? They have it so easy and they pick on me. I mean, why are these guys in a class with a bunch of freshmen, anyway? So they can pick on us? Allen said some of them don't need any more credits, so they take PE classes all day. What's the point in that? So they can make kids like me miserable?

I can hear Robb's voice in my head. I'll probably hear it in my sleep. When mom came in my room last night, I had to pretend I was asleep so she wouldn't know I had been crying.

Tuesday, 9-5

Please Don't Read This Page

Today's my birthday—I just turned fifteen. One more year till I can get my driver's license! Every birthday since I can remember, Mom measures my height. It's a ritual for my sister and me. I measured 5'5"—two inches taller than last year. I'm glad Mom didn't make me stand on the scale. I haven't weighed myself since summer camp. Back then, I weighed close to two hundred; luckily, my counselor was the only one who saw the scale. He tried not to make a big deal out of it, but I could tell he felt bad for me. He gave me an extra dessert at dinner, which didn't help my weight, but did make me feel special at the time.

I'm in math class right now. It's sooooo boring. I had all this stuff last year. Some of the kids don't get it, so we have to go over everything again and again. They don't understand simple things like variables and properties. When Mr. L asked what twice a number transfers into, hardly anybody answered. Then he put a bunch of examples on the board and we had to write them all down. It's so easy—twice means times two, things like that.

I know all this stuff from last year because I had a really good teacher. Some of the kids act like they've never heard of algebra, but I know they have. They just want the teacher to go slow so they don't have to work as hard.

The class is so rude to Mr. L I feel sorry for him, even though he is the most boring teacher I've ever had. At least he has an interesting classroom with cool posters and real fossils lying around. He has an aquarium with goldfish and he lets us feed them since it's early in the morning. Why does he continue to answer all their stupid questions? Can't he see they're laughing behind his back? Nate Hammer does it just to show off. I know him because he went to the same middle school as me in the seventh grade. He hasn't changed at all. He still loves to make fun of people, especially me. His eyes sure did light up when he saw me walk into class. Probably like when a hawk sees a squirrel. A big squirrel.

He has a huge crush on Whitney Elliot. She's pretty and seems nice, too. I don't know what she sees in Nate, but she always smiles at him. Her face gets all red. He's what you'd call a jock—I call him a jerk, but he's the most popular guy in our class. I swear he tries to make my life miserable. "It's Slim Jim!" he said the first time he saw me in class. Everyone laughed.

"It's Not-So-Slimmy-Jimmy," another kid joked. The class laughed again. Mr. L. quieted everyone down and I just wanted to disappear.

This year I'm even bigger than last year. My parents don't say much about my weight, but I know they're worried. I don't understand why I'm so fat. My friends at youth group eat more than I do, but they never gain weight.

Mr. L. keeps yelling for everybody to shut up, but they keep talking anyway. He just shakes his head and closes his book. There's only a few minutes left, so I guess he thinks it's not worth it to keep yelling at everybody. Nate is smiling at me, but I pretend I don't notice. But it doesn't matter. Nate still won't leave me alone.

"What'd you have for breakfast, Fat Boy? All of McDonald's? What're you writing? Listing all the food you're going to have for lunch?" Now the rest of the class is laughing. "You cause an earthquake every time you walk."

Ha, ha, Nate, you're so funny.

One minute till the bell rings...hurry and ring...please ring...Mr. L. acts like he doesn't hear what Nate's saying. I wonder if Whitney is laughing too.

Glad I didn't tell anybody it's my birthday.

Wednesday, 9-5

I'm so excited! I got a Wii for my birthday and it's awesome!

I got Super Smash Brothers Brawl and it is so sweet. You fight other players with tons of characters. Depending on whether or not you use the best finishing moves, you can open up better characters as you move through the game. My favorite is Captain Falco because he does this move where he teleports onto the opposite side of the screen. But Roy is pretty good too! He has this attack where you can throw one of his flaming swords at the other dude. You can cause major damage with that move, and it's almost impossible to defend against.

I can't wait to go home and see who else I can get. Maybe the teachers will give us a break and not give us so much homework, because my parents said I have to get done with that before I can play. Maybe my English teacher won't give us a lot to read tonight. Hint, hint.

Mom made fried chicken and dumplings last night, and then my favorite cake—German chocolate—topped with Moose Tracks ice cream from the United Dairy Farmers. I ate so much I could hardly move. On Saturday, my Nana is taking me to the all-you-can-eat steakhouse, like she does every year for my birthday. My sister gave me a really cool Bengal's sweatshirt, but it's too small so I have to take it back. I hope it comes in an XXL, because I really like it.

Thursday, 9-7

Please Don't Read This Page

Paul doesn't think the boyfriend did it. He thinks it's some guy from another state, like Kentucky.

"Why Kentucky?" I asked.

"Because the body was dumped in the woods, and everyone knows Kentucky is full of woods." Paul's been on the Internet hunting for murderers in Kentucky. I don't know why he's so set on Kentucky when it could be somebody around here. We've decided to set up a fake MySpace account and pretend we're this really cute cheerleader. Paul suggested we put my sister's picture on it, and call her Starr. I don't think my sister's cute enough, but Paul thinks she's hot. We're hoping the killer will send us a "friend request," then we can start talking to him and eventually Starr will ask him if he wants to get together. We'll leave a note for him at the meeting place and ask him to write back, so we get a copy of his fingerprints. Then we'll turn him in. The only problem is, my sister's not the nose ring type, like Kimberly. So, maybe the guy isn't into preppy girls like my sister. Paul said it wouldn't be that hard to Photoshop a nose ring in.

I wonder if Kimberly had a hard time fitting in and that's why she pierced her nose. From the pictures on the news, she looks kinda big, almost as big as me. The police thought maybe she was pregnant, and that's why her boyfriend murdered her. But the autopsy showed she wasn't. Some of the kids at school are making jokes, saying her boyfriend killed her because she was fat or that she ate herself to death. Seems like fat jokes never stop, even after you're dead.

Friday, 9-8

Please Don't Read This Page

We had school pictures taken today–I really hate picture day. It's okay to get out of class but that's about all it's worth. Ever since middle school, when I started getting bigger, I have dreaded the long walk. I feel like Frodo walking to Mordor. It used to be fun waiting in line, watching everyone comb their hair or asking, "How do I look?" I guess about three years ago, I quit asking. I remember the first time someone answered with a smile and said, "Oh, you look great, Jimmy," but I could tell they didn't mean it. They wanted to say, "You look pretty fat, Jimmy."

Today was no different. I got real nervous waiting and once again, it felt like forever before it was my turn. There's not much I can do to make my hair look decent; it's curly and sticks out all over the place. I tried getting it all shaved off last summer, but that made my face look even fatter.

"Sign this," the picture-lady said. She shoved a form at me. "What grade are you in?"

"Ninth," I told her.

She looked up at me. "Oh, really. Well, sign this," she repeated.

I filled out the form and stood quietly in line behind a kid named Frank. There's not much to do except watch the person getting photographed. White screen, bright lights, just great, let's shine a big light on Not-So-Slimmy-Jimmy.

"All right kid, sit on the stool and face left."

I sat down.

"Other left."

"Yes, ma'am," I said.

"Your glasses are reflecting too much. Tilt your head."

I could feel everyone's eyes on me and I started sweating. I thought I could get in a quick wipe of my forehead and I raised my arm. Click!

"Don't move, sit still," the lady yelled at me.

Someone behind me giggled and then I heard, "I wonder if that's a wide-angle lens?"

Haha.

I hate picture day. I could use a tan. The lights make my face look like a big pillow with eyes. At least it's not like family pictures with my whole body showing. I'm not quite Mr. Photogenic, you know. Actually the only parts of me that would look good in a picture are my "tits," as the football players call them, but they'd only be good if they were superimposed on an aging model that has been liposuctioned to the point of hanging flesh.

So, then, the lady goes, "Tilt your head down," then, "Up a bit. Okay, hold it right there."

She took forever and my eyes were drying out. I couldn't stand it. Blink. Click. Oh, great.

"Gee." She glanced at my form. "Jimmy. Let's try again."

I actually thought about running out. I didn't want the pictures anyway.

"C'mon. We have lunch in thirty minutes," someone said.

Then another one: "Maybe she's taking his picture in stages. Like those panorama things."

All I could think was *Shut up! Shut up! Shut up!* The last "Shut up!" I blurted out. Click.

The lady gave up. Mom probably won't be buying these pictures.

"Retakes are in a month," the helper lady told me as I went out the door.

Yippee. I can't wait.

Sunday, 9-10

I don't know why Paul's parents won't let him have a cell phone. I mean, what's the point? They bought him a used PC and let him have the Internet. I think it's pretty lousy, especially now, since there's been a murder right near his house. What if the creep kidnaps Paul? He won't be able to call 911 or anything. I mean, every kid has a cell phone nowadays.

Even though he doesn't have a cell, Paul's still been spying on the murder site behind his house everyday, plus he found more information about Kimberly on the web, like the autopsy report. It said she was missing a bone in her throat—the hyoid bone—that can be critical in determining whether a person has been strangled or not. The report said there was no evidence of illegal drugs and that the rest of her body was intact. They still suspect the boyfriend, but I wonder how an eighteen-year-old kid could remove a bone from someone's throat, especially his girlfriend's. The Channel 12 News said he was a good athlete but only an average student. It appears she had sex recently, probably with him. Not his biggest worry, since he faces murder charges. He admitted he was with her the night she died, but still claims he didn't do it. Her mom and dad were on the news crying, holding up her senior picture.

Channel 19 played a video of Kimberly playing trombone with her school marching band. The nose ring doesn't fit with the marching band, but who knows. I mean, I'm in jazz band,

and even we don't wear nose rings. Most band kids I know are geeky, but to them I'm still the fat kid nobody calls.

Tuesday, 9-12

Please Don't Read This Page

Guess what? Paul and I are already getting hits on our MySpace site. We're making up all kinds of stuff for my sister's face to say. Some of it's really stupid, but pretty funny. Every other word she uses is "like" and she skips school all the time. She likes to make out and sneaks her parents' cigarettes. So far, no one has asked to meet her, but you can tell most of the guys are really interested. I've been listening to my sister when she's on the phone, and writing down things she says so I can put them on MySpace. Mom saw me writing and wanted to know what I was doing. I told her I was writing in my journal. "That's a strange place to write. It looked like you had your ear glued to your sister's door."

I started to make up something, but she stopped me. "Don't start anything with your sister. I'm watching you, Jimmy Winterpock." As Mom walked down the stairs, I heard my sister squeal, "Oh, that's so gross! I wish I could've seen his face!" Then my sister hung up and called another one of her girlfriends. I took more notes as she told the whole story about some girls who put a pile of dog mess, wrapped in newspaper, above the door of Chad Barron's porch, because he cheated on Halle Duncan. They had it set up so that when he opened the door it would fly all over the place. Amy Cacaro faked her voice and called Chad from a pay phone. She said she was a new neighbor and had a flat tire a few houses down the street.

She wondered if he could help her. The guy must be a complete idiot because he fell for it. Two other girls hid behind one of the neighbor's fences and saw the dog mess fall on Chad when he opened the door. They said it was hilarious. He was cussing and calling for his mom. I bet his parents were really mad.

That night Paul and I added the story to MySpace. We had Starr take credit for thinking up the dog mess and putting it on Chad's porch. Of course, we didn't use Chad's real name.

Every guy who wrote thought it was pretty funny that a girl could think up something so gross. All but one. He didn't think it was funny at all. He thought it was one nasty trick. Paul thought maybe this guy is the killer. I wasn't too sure. I thought he might be some undercover cop. That would be NOT good. Paul said that if it was a cop, he would be glad that we were trying to catch Kimberly's murderer.

Saturday, 9-16

At the beginning of every year, at least one teacher assigns an essay about summer vacation. So one day before school started I got really bored and decided to get a jump on my homework and write about something I did over the summer. Just my luck, the one year I have it ready, not one teacher asked me to write about my summer vacation. So, instead of wasting all that work, I decided to put it in this journal. You can grade it if you want, or give me extra credit for it, or something. I really worked hard on it. So, anyway, here is my essay.

My Summer Vacation in Gatlinburg

This past summer, my church youth group went to a conference in Gatlinburg, Tennessee, called Summer Jam.

It was really cool since we had so much to do. We could buy souvenirs, play laser tag, ride the go-carts, play miniature golf, or hang out in the amusement park. I love laser tag, and really pushed it, but all my friends wanted to go to the water park since it was so hot outside. I reminded them that if we played laser tag, the building would be air-conditioned, but that didn't change their minds, so my dad drove us to Splash Mountain Water Park.

Splash Mountain is a pretty sweet water park with a wave pool, a Lazy River, and water slides. It sounded really fun and exciting, but I don't really like to swim. I'm pretty big, especially in the chest and it's embarrassing for me to take my shirt off, not so much around my friends, but in front of strangers.

At first I just sat in a chair by the Lazy River. I was determined to stay out of the water, so no one would see how fat I was. Plus, I have to squint to see without my glasses. But, my friends kept encouraging me to get in the water, and in the end, I couldn't resist. I took off my shirt and thought, "I don't care what they think about me. It doesn't matter what people say." I kept repeating that to myself. Once my shirt was off, I heard some kid from another group say that I had the biggest chest of anyone he knew, girls included.

Later, when I got out of the Lazy River and headed towards one of the slides, the humiliation got worse. Kids I didn't even know laughed in my face and pointed at me. I heard one say that he bet the water level went up when I got in. You would think they would at least wait until I passed by them to say anything. They acted like I was a clown hired by the park to entertain everyone. I suppose I should have played along with their jokes and shook my body around, acting silly, but that's not who I am. I don't like being the center of attention so I rode down one slide and then hid in the wave pool. My friends felt bad that I was by myself, and told me to ignore the other kids, but I couldn't. The rest of the trip went okay, but I didn't go swimming again. Neither did my friends. We did play laser tag, but it wasn't as much fun as I remembered.

Monday, 9-18

Paul hates Northview. He says the kids are all a bunch of geeks, and he usually skips lunch because the cafeteria is so gross. I don't mind school, but I don't have too many friends. At least I have Allen and Spencer to sit with at the lunch table. I forgot to mention Spencer, a new kid from Montana that moved to my street. He's a freshman like me. My mother really likes his mom, and they kind of introduced us to each other. He rides the bus home from school sometimes with us, but his dad takes him in the mornings. He's Mormon and has to get up earlier than most kids and have seminary. I think that's a special prayer meeting or something. He's really athletic and is going to try out for the soccer team. He has lunch the same period as Allen and me, so I asked him if he wanted to sit with us. He's really cool, and I noticed the girls try to talk to him all the time. Spencer told Allen and me he played club soccer in Montana and hopes to get a college scholarship. I don't play soccer anymore because I can't run very fast. I tried this summer to play in a club league, but all the other kids made fun when I ran after the ball, and I saw some of the parents pointing. So I decided I'd rather be in jazz band and play the sax.

Wednesday, 9-20

Allen is such a brainless kid. Spencer and I really gave it to him during lunch today. I mean, he walked to the table, well, I wouldn't really call it walking, I would have to call it waddling, like he had on high heels or something. As soon as we saw him, Spencer said, "Man, what's wrong with you? You look like you messed in your pants."

Allen grinned like he always does. "Somebody just stuck a pencil down my butt-cheeks. I have to dump my stuff before I can get it out." He had a funny look on his face. Then he put his tray on the table and reached down the back of his pants. I could see the tables behind him laughing their heads off. But what made matters even worse, he pulled out the pencil and placed it on the table, right next to our food. That about made me and Spencer puke. Finally, Spencer couldn't take it any more. "Dude! Get rid of that freaking thing! You don't just toss it on the table like it's just any pencil. That thing is contaminated. What's with you, man?"

While Allen was at the trash can, Spencer talked to me about him. "We have to tell him how to wear his pants. He doesn't have a clue sometimes."

"Tell me about it," I said to Spencer, while shaking my head. I mean, Spencer's right. Allen wears these big pants that hang halfway down his cheeks, and when he bends over you have a clear view of his crack. I've seen kids throw spit wads down the back of his pants, and act like they're making a "basket." Allen has so much fat, he doesn't even feel it.

So, we both told Allen to get some pants that fit, and I threw in that he needed to get some shirts that fit, and shoes other than Hush Puppies. "I mean, those look like they belong to some old man."

Allen just looked at me with his fish eyes, and said, "They did. They're my grandpa's shoes. He died last year, and my grandmother gave me his shoes cause they're my size. I like wearing them."

"Are those your grandpa's pants too?" Spencer asked.

"Yeah," said Allen. "But I have some that don't hang so far down." He scratched his butt. "That pencil didn't feel too good."

"Then why are you smiling about it?" Spencer asked him. "We can live with the shoes but the pants have got to go. I will never look at a pencil the same again." We didn't say anything more to him about his clothes. If the kid missed his grandpa enough to wear his clothes, then his grandpa must have been a pretty good guy. There's no getting people. Just when you think you have them all figured out, they do something that just blows your mind, if you know what I mean.

We might go to the movies this weekend if there's something good playing. If not, maybe we can go back to our old neighborhood. That would be nice. I miss my old house.

Saturday, 9-23

Please Don't Read This Page

Paul and I hung out today. At first my parents were reluctant to let me go to his house, because of the murder, but I promised I wouldn't do anything stupid. Besides, the police are pretty sure it was the boyfriend, probably an argument or something, and he just freaked. It's really kinda sad, because the kid's a good baseball player and the scouts have been watching him for the last year. He doesn't look like the violent type. Even though he's the number one suspect, I feel sorry for him.

The murder site was all roped off with yellow tape, so Paul and I couldn't even get close to it. A few police were there. They had on suits and were walking around with notepads. We walked along the ravine across from the site and looked for stuff the murderer might have dropped. All we found were a few cigarette butts and an empty beer can. We hid in the old shed behind Paul's house and took turns watching out the window with binoculars for the murderer, but no one showed up and we got bored. Paul's mom ordered pizza for us, and we added some more stuff to our fake MySpace. Paul had the bright idea of making Starr real slutty. Paul thought it would be cool if she talked about tongue kissing and how big her boobs are. I think it's kind of cheesy, but Paul says we're desperate. We need to find the murderer before Kimberly's boyfriend gets fried in the electric chair. Paul found a model with big breasts and Photoshopped them onto my sister's picture. I thought it was a dumb idea to change the picture right in the middle of everything. Paul said it was for the new guys clicking in.

Friday, 9-29

I've never been to a pep rally before and since everyone else was excited about it, I was too. In our last period class, the assistant principal called us to the gym by grades. Of course, the freshmen were last and so by the time we got there, most of the seats were taken. Teachers were yelling at us to go sit down but it was just a big wad of students, which was mostly us freshmen not knowing what to do. "Hurry, sit down, we need to start," they kept hollering at us. I don't know what the problem was, but I got caught in a bunch of people at the top of the steps and then everyone behind me pushed forward. My feet got hung on the person in front of me and I tripped. So, if you saw all the commotion over in the freshmen section, that was me knocking about ten people over. I couldn't help it but they all got mad at me anyway. I told them someone pushed me. And I bruised my leg on the bleachers. The teachers in the area tried to restore order but it didn't work. One of them said for me to watch what I was doing, I could hurt someone. It was pointless to respond so I just said, "Yes, ma'am," and sat down.

What I got to see of the pep rally was fun. They blindfolded a senior and had him crawl around on the gym floor trying to find $10 and $20 bills. Every time he got close to one, the whole place would scream and he'd get all frantic and go right by the money. It was really funny. Then the cheerleaders did a cheer and threw candy to the class that yelled the loudest. When it was our turn to yell, all of us freshmen just sat there while the rest of the school booed. It's like we're not even part of the school, like we're only there for other students to make fun of. It's going to be a long year.

Then the football players ran out of the locker room and jumped around and bumped chests together. We all cheered. Right in the middle of them was Robb Thuman. In case you really aren't reading my turned down pages, Robb's in my PE class and I sit next to him in the locker room. Even though he's a senior, he talks with me sometimes along with some of his buddies. I hope they win tonight so he'll be in a good mood on Monday.

About five minutes before we were supposed to leave, a bunch of students got up and started walking out of the gym. No matter what the teachers said, it became a flood of people; nothing could've stopped everyone from leaving. The band was still playing and the football players were still talking on the microphone about the game that night. I had to catch the bus, so I got in the middle of the crowd and headed up the stairs. Some kid I knew in 6th grade and who is good friends with Nate saw me. He had a big smile on his face. He said, "Nice going, Winterpock. Saw you bowl over half the ninth grade." He and his buddies had a good laugh.

We just finished dinner and Mom asked me if I was going to the game. It's at home and we play the Eagles from Academy. I told her I didn't feel too good and that I'd go to the next home game. Besides, I have to practice my sax.

Monday, 10-2

I have tests in almost all my classes this Friday. I don't know why every teacher thinks they have to give tests on Friday. Why not Tuesday or Wednesday sometimes? It's like they think, "Ooops, it's Friday, I better give a test, because everybody else is giving one." Talk about peer pressure.

Oh, I forgot to tell you: Spencer made the first cut for the JV fall soccer team, which is great for a freshman. Especially a new kid. He was all excited about it on the bus ride home. He starts practice tomorrow, so he won't be on the bus with us until the season's over. I noticed the kids don't pick on Allen and me as much because of Spencer. Everyone thinks he's really cool. Even Whitney. He's so lucky to have the hottest girl chasing him. I feel proud that someone like him hangs out with Allen and me; Spencer has a lot of courage. Allen complains about him though. He says it's been taking Spencer longer and longer to get to our lunch table—he spends a lot of time hanging out with the jocks and some of the cheerleaders. I hope he doesn't become one of them, but if he does, I don't blame him. If he hangs around with Allen and me, he might catch whatever disease we have, which I guess is the "laughed at" disease.

It's funny how you can be in the middle of several hundred people and feel like you're lost in some kind of a jungle. Kind of like it's Survivor—The Lunch Room.

We got a couple of new students in math class this week. Whenever we get another new kid in class, the teachers get all freaked and act like it's the worst thing in the world to add another name in their grade book. I guess I don't blame them. In some classes we're up to thirty-five students. The teachers miss half of what's going on, and kids cheat like crazy. Mr. L still doesn't know my name, and it's been way over two weeks since school's started. If that's not enough, the teacher ran out of books in social studies. Welcome to high school.

Friday, 10-6

Please Don't Read This Page

My sister came home all upset today. She was crying and screaming that her life is ruined, and she can never face her friends again. Which, by the way, isn't true. Her friends have been calling her non-stop. You'd think they'd get sick of listening to her boo-hoo about her stupid life. When I asked Mom about it, she stared at me so hard I could actually feel the heat.

"What?" I asked.

"You better not have had anything to do with this," she said.

"Do with what? Somebody clue me in please."

"This!" my sister screamed as she slammed down the phone, holding up a piece of printer paper.

When I saw what was on it, I almost gagged on my Little Debbie. There was Starr with her super-sized chest. At that moment I wanted to murder Paul. Why did he have to make them so freaking big?

"Someone found this on the Internet, and now there are copies all around school."

"How could I have missed that?" I said.

"Because you're a brainless idiot!" she screamed. She grabbed a soda out of the refrigerator and then shoved the door closed. "I will kill the asshole who did this too me! I'll claw out his eyes!"

"Watch your language, young lady," Mom said, as she took the picture from Jessica. "Who would do this?" She cut her eyes at me.

I leaned over Mom's shoulder, pretending I had never seen the picture. "Pretty good likeness, I think."

Jessica punched me in the arm, really hard. "You don't understand, Mom. The jerk who did this wrote things about me. Now everyone knows about Chad..." Jessica caught herself.

"Chad?" Mom raised her left eyebrow.

"Oh, nothing! Just nothing!" Then she screamed like a cave woman. "Auuuuugh! I'm going to find out who did this. And when I do...Just wait!"

"How do you know it's a 'he'?" I asked. "Could be one of your loser girlfriends."

"Maaaaahm! Make him shut up!" she hollered as she ran upstairs, no doubt to get on the phone and talk about it for another two hours.

"What makes you think you can catch the person?" I yelled up at her.

She stopped and turned around. "Because Danny Miller broke into the School Board's website last year. And he said he'd find out who did this, and when he does, I'll make sure the jerk pays big time." Then she started crying again. "Every time someone passes me in the hall, I wonder, 'Is that who did this to me?' It's awful, I can't trust anyone."

"Gee, that's tough," I said. "I'm really sorry." She had no idea how sorry I was. "Let me know if I can help."

"Where are you going?" Mom eyed me suspiciously as I slinked up the stairs.

"I'm swamped with homework."

Mom directed her attention to Jessica. "Well, honey, I'm sure whoever did this knows how bad you feel, and how much trouble they're in now. This is probably the end of all this nonsense. I'm sure that awful site will disappear. In fact, I'm sure it will be gone by tomorrow."

I couldn't get up the stairs fast enough. I had the weird feeling Mom knew I had something to do with Jessica's enhanced photo. As soon as I got to my room, I called Paul and told him the whole thing.

"No kidding, she found out?"

"We're such idiots," I said. "Why didn't we realize that someone she knew would recognize her picture?"

"Does that mean we need to delete the site?"

"Well, duh," I said.

"Well, you might want to think twice about getting rid of it. At least right away. We're starting to get tons of requests and the blog's really taking off. She's getting some good e-mails. Let's stay with it for a few more weeks. I just know we're getting close."

"Okay, but if we don't get something in two weeks, we're closing it down. My sister has a friend who's a really good hacker. If she ever finds out, there'll be another body in the woods. Mine."

"Don't worry, no one's that good."

Tuesday, 10-10

I have Mr. Mackey for Physical Science. He thinks he's funny but mostly he's goofy. He does show us some cool things in lab every now and then. Today, he asked Jeff Murray to help him with a demonstration. Mr. M took a rubber hose and attached it to the gas jets and stuck a small funnel in the other end of the hose. He had a tray of liquid soap, like for making bubbles, and he dipped the funnel in it. Then he turned on the gas and blew a bubble. Lying on the counter was a yardstick with a lit candle taped to one end. What he did next was pretty cool. He twisted the funnel with a bubble on the end of it so that the bubble came off and floated in the air. The bubble was full of gas and he grabbed the candle on the stick and poked the bubble. A big whoosh of flame went off in the middle of the room. It was sweet! We all hollered for him to do it again. That's when he got Jeff up there to help. Jeff is always messing up things, and I think Mr. M thought he could do the candlestick part and look good in front of the class. How hard could it be? Mr. Mackey told him to wait until the bubble was up in the air but Jeff couldn't wait. He got so excited that he pushed the candle into the funnel before the bubble even got shook off of it. Our teacher jumped back when the ball of flame covered his hands, and he yelled "Holy Crap!" right in front of us. Some people in class laughed but stopped when they saw the hair burned off of Mr. Mackey's forearm. It stunk too. I don't think Jeff will be in any more demos.

After that craziness I went to math class. Mr. L had promised to tell us the answer to the riddle about the twenty-six sheep and how many were left. He made us guess again but he still shook his head at our answers. I'm pretty good at math and I had to know. He said that we might be in the wrong class if we can't do simple subtraction like this. When he told us that it was nineteen, I couldn't believe it. "How?" we all screamed. Then he said, "Well, if there were twenty and they were all sick and one died, wouldn't that be nineteen? You know, twenty *sick* sheep."

We felt like a big bunch of suckers. He just laughed at his joke the rest of the period.

After that, the day was pretty normal. As normal goes for me. We lost the game Friday, so PE was about the same. Robb, the one football player that I sit near in the locker room, said his little brother got knocked down by some big goof at the pep rally. He said it better not have been me. I wanted to say, "Nice game Friday," but I didn't. I'm not that stupid.

Wednesday, 10-11

Please Don't Read This Page

At Youth Group tonight, Paul pulled me aside to talk about our undercover operations. A few kids started to walk toward us, so Paul and I slinked out of the room and down the hall near the restroom. After we looked around the corner to make sure the coast was clear, Paul filled me in on the latest website hits.

"That guy who's been e-mailing Starr wrote today saying he wants to meet her. He says he lives in Hanover! Jimmy, it could be him, the killer! 'Starr' agreed to meet him after school tomorrow—at Starbucks by the mall. The one in Barnes and Noble. Around 4:00."

"No way, man." Suddenly all this detective work made me queasy. "We're going to get caught, or be arrested or worse."

"Or catch the murderer. He won't know it's us. Remember, he's looking for some girl. Your sister, but with big hooters."

I shook my head. "I don't know. Now this seems crazy."

"We've got to go through with it, Jimmy. We could catch the killer and get the boyfriend off the hook," Paul told me.

"What if he starts shooting or something?"

"For what, because his latte is too hot? He'll just leave if Starr doesn't show up. And we won't be there if you chicken out."

I thought about it and decided we could end up famous. Maybe I'd even be popular for a change. "Okay, I'm in."

<u>Thursday, 10-12</u>

Please Don't Read This Page

Paul is such a doofus. He almost got us killed today. In case you really are reading this, if you tell anybody about what happened, you will be the cause of my death.

You may have noticed I was not paying attention like I usually do. All I could think of all day was the big meeting with the killer. The guy e-mailed Starr that he would be wearing a Sea World baseball hat. That should have been clue number one. I mean, would a murderer wear a hat with Shamu on it?

Anyway, after school, Paul and I rode our bikes to the Barnes and Noble where Starbucks is—we got there a half an hour early, so we could sit in the back. We took some homework and bought drinks so it would look like we were really doing something. Our plan was to wait for him to order coffee. We figured he'd drink his coffee and wait; then when no one showed up, he'd leave. That's when we'd take his cup and give it to the police to see if his fingerprints matched those from the murder scene. Paul brought his dad's digital camera. I'd stand near the guy and Paul would act like he was taking my picture, but really take his. We were ready.

Here's what actually happened. We parked our bikes out front in case we had to make a quick getaway. I ordered an iced caramel macchiato and Paul got a white chocolate mocha. We sat way in the back so we could watch the door without being noticed. Paul about drove me crazy fooling with the camera. The flash kept going off and the people trying to read and talk got mad at us. After about a half hour, a few girls walked in, giggling. They looked like some of my sister's friends, but I couldn't be sure. Then some guys came in, but none had on the right hat. I was so busy looking at their hats I didn't realize that one of the guys was Danny Miller. I started to get nervous. Really nervous.

"Calm down, dude," Paul said. "He's not wearing the hat, is he?"

Then we saw it. A hat with a big Sea World on it. Some guy from school. The one my sister has a big crush on. Then I saw my sister peeking in the window. She waited a few seconds, and then she opened the door and walked in.

"Oh, crap!" I whispered loudly. "It's Jessica. Let's get out of here." I spun around in my chair before she saw me.

"There's only one way out, nitwit, and that's through the front door."

My sister and her friends were looking around for a place to sit. "Quick, let's hide in the bathroom," I said. We grabbed our books and drinks and, keeping our heads down, snaked our way to the back of the bookstore.

"This sucks," said Paul after he was safe inside his stall. "Why can't we hide in the books somewhere? Or hang out in the music section until they leave?"

"No way. I don't want to take any chances. I'm staying right here—behind a locked door. Man, my head's buzzing from the caffeine."

"Quit complaining. Don't you understand the deep pile of crap we're in? Ha, get it? Deep crap we're in? Man, what are you doing over there? It's smells like elephant farts."

"They're not as bad as my grandpa's. They're sick."

"Never heard of anyone inheriting farts."

"Hey, what if one of them crawls underneath the door?"

"Why would anyone do that? Like, 'Hey, I think I'll crawl under the door to see who's in there. Might be fun to see some dude squatting on porcelain.' Get real, man."

Then a toilet flushed. "Paul," I whispered. "I hope that was you."

"Don't worry, I was just testing the equipment. There's nothing else to do in here."

Paul kept sneaking out to see if my sister and her friends had left yet, but it seemed they weren't in a hurry to go anywhere. My sister wanted revenge in a big way, and she was willing to wait for it.

"What if she stays here until they close," Paul said. "We can't stay in here forever."

"There's no way we can let my sister see us together. She'll know we did it. Then my life is as good as over. If she finds out, I'll have to run away."

"She can't stay that much longer. What time do you have to be home?" Paul asked.

"Mom expects us home for dinner at 6:30."

"What time is it now?"

"Ten after four."

"That's just great. We only have two more hours in here."

We were glad it wasn't that crowded—we didn't have to give up our stalls for anybody. Danny Miller came in once, and we watched him check out his muscles through the thin opening in the door. It actually was pretty funny, and Paul and I had a good laugh about it later. Every fifteen minutes Paul would sneak out of the bathroom to see if my sister and her friends were still there. They didn't leave until twenty after six. We waited a few more minutes to make sure they were gone.

By the time I got home, it was dark and Mom was fuming. "I've been worried sick and so has Mrs. Grove. Where were you?"

"Yeah, where were you?" my sister asked, her head tilted a bit like she was already suspicious. I had to be real cool or I would end up banned from my own family.

"We rode our bikes to the mall and went to GameStop. Guess we lost track of time. Sorry, Mom."

"Sorry? Is that all you have to say for yourself? Sorry? Didn't you know what time it was?"

"I saw a couple of bikes at Starbucks," my sister said.

"And your point?" I said. "So, you saw a couple of bikes at Starbucks. What does that have to do with anything?" I was barely floating. And talking too much.

"Well, one looked just like yours." She was looking at me but I didn't look back.

"Do you know how many bikes out there look like mine?"

"I think you know something, you weasel."

"Okay, you two, that's enough," Dad said. "Jimmy, you can forget going anywhere for two weeks. Now let's eat, we've been waiting on you long enough."

All through dinner my sister asked me one stupid question after another. Like what kind of bike does Paul have, and how could both of us lose track of time, and why did I pick this particular day to go to the mall. She was annoying everybody at the table and Dad finally told her to leave me alone. Mom, though, kept looking back and forth between me and Jessica, like she was figuring something out. It was really eerie. Like she was using some sixth sense so she'd know exactly what was going on.

That night when I finally went to my room, I erased Starr's MySpace page.

Please Don't Read This Page

It has been such a long week, it feels like it's been a month. Jessica's still upset, and Mom's barely speaking to me. I've pretty much stayed out of both their ways. Dad's kept himself scarce too. I've been a wreck all day with it being Friday the 13th. I've been waiting for one of my sister's friends to say something about seeing Paul and me in Starbucks. But so far, no one's said anything.

Paul's coming over tonight—it's been planned since last week, but Mom's acting funny about it. Dad's on my side. He thinks Mom's treating me unfairly. "Jimmy shouldn't be punished because Jessica's unhappy," I heard him say to Mom. "He needs to have a life, and friends. Paul's an okay kid. You know what his home life is like, Mare."

Mom murmured something under her breath, and Dad gave me the "it's okay" sign.

Even with the "okay" sign from Dad, I told Paul to cool it about the murder in front of my parents and Jessica. Especially Jessica. He's still obsessed with the murder though. He reads everything he can about it and watches the news all the time. Paul swears he can tell if someone is innocent or guilty by the look in their eyes. The boyfriend, Paul says, has that "they-think-I'm-guilty-but-I'm-innocent" look. Paul says he knows that look, because his dad's always accusing him of things he didn't do, like smoking pot and sneaking booze.

"Okay, the Starr thing didn't work out," Paul said. "But there has to be some way to catch the killer."

"No way, man," I said. "Count me out. I'm not spending

another minute in a bathroom stall, unless I have to."

"Don't worry. I found something much better. Doesn't involve anybody in our family. I found these really cool Internet sites that identify sexual predators in neighborhoods."

"I don't believe what I'm hearing."

"We need to check all the areas surrounding Wilmington High. It might take a while, but I think the guy must have been stalking Kimberly for a long time, so he's got to live around her neighborhood somewhere."

"I thought you said the murderer was from Kentucky."

"Not any more. There's too much evidence that he's from around here."

"Like what?"

"Like the cigarette butts we found near the murder site. And the stalking."

"Couldn't someone from Kentucky be a stalker?"

"I thought about that, but the police said it must be someone nearby who knows her. And knows her habits," Paul said.

"That's what I thought to begin with, then you came up with this goofy Kentucky theory."

Paul was quiet for a second. "Yeah, well it could still be someone from Kentucky, but we have a better chance if it's someone from around here, so I thought we'd try that first. If it doesn't work, then we'll start looking in Kentucky."

"Or, we could play Super Smash and just let the police take care of it."

But I knew Paul wasn't going to let it go.

Monday, 10-16

The weekend started out pretty good. We got a new dog, a golden retriever—he's only eight weeks old and is really hyper. My sister named him Taffy; it's an okay name, but I would have named him something less girlie, like Snoop Doggie or Apollo. But I got to name Nanook, our other dog, so Mom let Jessica name the new one. I think Mom's hoping the new puppy will help Jessica get over her humiliation. It seems to be working. It's hard to stay miserable around such a funny dog. You can be in the middle of playing a game with him, like tug-o-war, and he just falls asleep. He's crazy.

Paul spent the night Friday. I was worried about Mom, but she acted okay. All she did was worry about the dog chewing the furniture and peeing on the carpet. At first Paul and I played video games. He likes Super Smash Brothers but it isn't his favorite. What he really wanted to do was talk about the murder. We stayed up till almost three surfing the web and found over two hundred sex predators in Hanover County. I couldn't believe it. We never expected to find that many—maybe one or two, but two hundred? That's pretty scary. We decided to check our streets, but didn't find anyone. It makes you realize how hard it is for the police to solve a case, with so many criminals out there. The whole thing was really discouraging. Unless the guy really screws up, it'll be a long time before he gets caught, if he ever does. Paul's not giving up though. He thinks most criminals slip up; we just have to figure out how. He hasn't been able to spy on the murder site as much as he wants because his dad's been on his case about it. His dad told him he'd "kick his ass" if he found him snooping around there anymore. Which means I'm not snooping around there either.

Saturday morning Dad took Paul home. I just sat around the rest of the day watching TV. Dad watched the baseball game—the Reds stink again. "They can't pitch or hit or run," he said. I don't care about the game as much as I like collecting baseball cards. Soccer's better, and I've always wanted to play for the school, like Spencer does. Like that would ever happen. I played hockey when I was in fifth grade, but I wasn't fast, so the coach made me a backup goalie.

Some of the guys in my PE class are soccer players; a couple are from somewhere in South America. So far, they're a lot nicer than the football players.

Tuesday, October 17

School today was a pain. We're preparing for testing, so in English (as you know!) and math we had to review stuff we've been studying for years. If I have to cross-multiply one more time, I might puke. It's so boring and I don't know why some people never get it. I guess we all have our problems.

Mom made me turkey sandwiches for lunch but I bought pizza too. The cafeteria also has these chocolate-chip cookies that they make each day. They're soft and when they just come out of the oven, they are so good. I can eat my two and if someone doesn't want theirs, I get those too. One day last week, I put some extra cookies in my book bag for later and forgot about them. When I got home, they had soaked through and got chocolate stains all over the living room carpet where I threw my bag. Mom was so mad at me.

<u>Thursday, October 19</u>

Hi, Ms. Pope. I'm in class working on my Comparison / Contrast paper. You said it was optional whether we do a Venn diagram. I'm going to write about my two neighborhoods. You said you would look it over and make comments before we hand in the final draft.

Hopewell Court vs. Chesdin Circle

The summer had finally come and you could smell the freedom in the air. It was so wonderful, yet we were moving away from 13838 Chesdin Circle.

My family had been looking at houses since January. My sister, Jessica, was in the tenth grade, and my parents decided that if we were going to move, we should move before she started another year in high school. We had some friends that moved to Hanover a few years before and they seemed to like it.

Mom and Dad wanted to leave our old neighborhood, Adams Farms, because it had turned upside down. My parents said that it was once a respected place to live. I thought if that was true then I'm Elvis Presley, because it's not even close to that now. There are gangs all around the neighborhood and my mom doesn't like the school district very much. She worked with the school so she knew what went on there. She compared Hanover's test scores with Adams's test scores. Adams wasn't even in the chase!

One fateful night my mom and dad made a decision that would change my life forever. We were moving. I thought, "Hey, this might be kind of cool." However, at that time I had no clue how much of an impact it would have on my life. It hadn't sunk in yet that in two months I would be a thirty-minute drive from all that I've ever known. From the only house I've ever lived in. I was in major denial.

So, we started looking at houses and finally found one we liked. We thought it would be the perfect home. Apparently, God had different plans for us and someone outbid us. Luckily, we found another house near our first choice. When I heard that we actually bought a house in Hanover, I was bouncing off the walls like a maniac, I was so happy. However, many happy things come to an end.

The next day when I started to gather things from my room to put in our new house, it sunk in. I felt terrible and wished we were not leaving. I thought about my friends, my teachers and all the memories. "We're going to move," I whispered to myself. "We're going to move."

The rest of the day I kept to myself while my family tried to cheer me up. It was a miserable day as all of my memories came back to me. Good, bad, funny and sad memories came back to me that day, no matter how little or insignificant they were. I just couldn't get over the fact that we were moving. "Will I ever see my friends again?" I thought. I didn't have many friends, but at least I had some. I wondered if I would find even one friend at my new school.

I woke up to reality and tried to deal with it as best I could. I helped move stuff into the new house, and helped my sister with her belongings. Within a week we were all moved in. I waved a final farewell to my friends at Adams Farms, and then I was out of there.

So now I have been here for two months. I still talk on the phone to my old friends, but not very often. My mom and dad are happy with my school and our neighborhood. Even though I'm trying to fit in, I still wish that we had never moved.

The End.

Friday, 10-20

Please Don't Read This Page

Today I was in the gym when it started again with the guys in the locker room. Of course, there's never anyone around, but I don't want teachers to have to protect me. I'd like to fight back but I know I'd get pounded on big time. "Melon Boy" and "Man-Boobs," they yell at me. I hate it and it makes my neck turn red. The worst is Robb. He apparently comes to school for the purpose of playing football and making my life miserable. Most of the time he starts it and then the others join in. Today, he said, "Hey, Jimmy, are you gellin', because I see your melons!" He has figured out that talking about my chest really bugs me. But he doesn't care. As long as he's getting laughs, he just keeps on going. He's like the Energizer Jerk. And then I find out Nate's been switched to my PE class. He laughs harder than anyone when Robb starts in on me. I can take the teasing about me being too big, but when the jokes about my chest start up, I just crumble inside. The more they say those things, the more I believe that what they say is true. That I don't care. That I am fat and lazy.

It's interesting how the sermon this past Sunday seemed to be speaking to me. It made me wonder if my parents had said something to the preacher. He opened his Bible and talked about Peter 3:3-4. It's the part about inner beauty and how it doesn't matter what you're like on the outside. What counts is on the inside.

I have a good heart and try to treat people right, but it seems everybody worries more about how you look. When we're in line at the grocery store, every magazine has all these pictures of beautiful women and muscle men and movie stars. Then I look down at myself or I catch someone looking at me and I cringe. But it helps to hear my preacher talk about these things. Otherwise, I would get really depressed. I just wish some of the kids in gym class could hear what he says.

Sunday, 10-22

Saturday, I had to rake and rake and rake leaves. Man, was it a lot. I never knew there were that many leaves on a tree. Me and Dad started at 9 in the morning and didn't finish until noon. At first it was cold and I could see my breath but then I got hot from working. Mom brought us some hot chocolate. By the time we finished there was a pile of leaves as big as a car. Tomorrow, we'll burn them in the back corner. I did fall in the pile once, just like when I was little. My lazy sister didn't help at all. She sat on the sofa and talked on the phone. I think she should major in communications when she goes to college.

Mom made a pot of chili for lunch. She makes it with mushrooms, peppers and big hamburger chunks. I ate three bowls while watching the UC game. I have some homework to do, which includes re-writing an essay for your class (Remember, the one on pollution you marked up with your "screamin' demon" red pen?), reading a chapter in history and then some math homework. Actually, I need to study for a math test. Who gives tests on Monday? Someone who doesn't care about students, that's who. I hope you're not planning on doing that anytime soon. Like ever. If you do, then I take it back. I know you care about us.

Maybe this week, I'll go to the football game. It's homecoming and I want to see if the girl I voted for wins. My sister's friend Asha is on the court but she is such a snob, she doesn't deserve to win. She came over today and when I walked in the TV room, she said, "Freshmen make me sick." I said she could always leave. My sister asked if I had something to do that didn't involve being at home. I went to my room and played video games. When my sister is mean or lets her friends be mean, I really enjoy hunting for aliens. If there was some way to put Jessica's face on the monster, I would.

I'll try and talk Allen into going to the game so I can sit with someone. If Asha doesn't win, I can't wait for her to come back over to our house.

Tuesday, 10-24

I heard Mom talking on the phone with Mrs. Johnson from where we used to live. I might get to go back there for Halloween and go trick-or-treating with my old friends. That would be too cool. If I can't, I probably won't go at all—it's no fun to walk around if you don't know anyone. Mom would insist on following me and I would be so embarrassed. This year, I want to be the dad from *The Incredibles*. Mom is good about making my outfits if I give her enough time. One year, she waited until the last couple of days before trying to make my Spiderman outfit. It came out a little small and I wore it anyway. I was standing in front of this one house and I bent over to get a Reese's and my pants ripped. I couldn't hear because of my mask, so for the rest of the night, every time I walked away from someone's door, they would start laughing. It wasn't until Mom ran into our old next door neighbor at the grocery store that I even found out.

Wednesday, 10-25

Tonight was youth group night at church. We don't always go to church on Wednesday but I'm glad we did this time. With all the video games we have at church, I have a good time playing the other kids. You would think church would be boring but I always enjoy it a lot. We even have our own band and it's awesome. Last night we played some really good tunes. I was bummed Paul didn't show up, because we really smoke when we're playing the sax together. I don't get it. He lives for youth group—at least that's what he told me. I think it's this whole murder thing. That's all he thinks about. I'm beginning to think he's afraid that the murderer will come after him, since it happened so near his house.

It might sound like all I do at church is play games and practice with our band, but we have classes and the preacher talks to us. It's a bit more relaxed on Wednesday than on Sunday. One game that I love is Foosball and we have one at church. I can twirl the men really hard. A few weeks ago, I was playing when I spun the thing so fast it kicked the ball across the room and under the ping-pong table. Sable Moore—the same one that's in our English class—went to get it and crawled halfway under there. Right when she reached for the ball she saw a bug or something that moved and she screamed and raised up. Her head bonked into the table and that made her squeal again. Everyone came running. Then we got yelled at for being too loud. It was way too much fun.

Going to church on Wednesday really helps me get revived for the rest of the week. I can't wait till next week. Maybe Paul will be there. I have to go do some other homework now, but I hope you're reading our journals. I didn't think I would like doing this but it's okay for something I have to do. I have to admit that even though you aren't supposed to be reading the ones we tell you not to, I like writing them. It makes me feel like I have a good friend that listens. Even if it's just me.

Saturday, 10-28

I went to the game last night, mostly because I wanted to see who won Homecoming Queen. Allen went with me and his dad took us. Before the game, the cheerleaders rode the floats around the track and threw candy and little plastic footballs into the crowd. I almost caught one, but Allen knocked my arm and some kid behind me got it.

The theme for this year was "Reach for the Stars," but it should have been "Let's Boo and Terrorize the Freshmen Float." Ours was first in line and I admit that it was pretty cheesy. We had a cardboard cutout of a space shuttle and some kid dressed up like an astronaut, but the problem was that he couldn't see out of his helmet, and he was waving toward the football field instead of the crowd. The man driving the float wasn't paying attention to the cars in front of him, and he had to stop real quick. He hit the brakes and all the people on the float went flying forward. Everyone in the stands laughed. Then the astronaut kid couldn't get up, and when he did, he head-butted a cheerleader's rear end and knocked her down again. That was really funny. When our float got in front of the senior section, the seniors started throwing the candy back at our float. The cheerleaders got behind the space shuttle, but the astronaut got hit with a little football right on top of his head. When that happened, all the seniors went crazy cheering.

It was exciting when our team finally ran through the big banner onto the field. Parkwood is either really bad or we're better than I thought, cause we were way ahead by halftime. Robb Thuman started as quarterback, and he played awesome during the first half. Maybe it's okay that he picks on me.

Just before halftime, me and Allen went to get some popcorn and a hotdog. Nate and his dad were in line behind us, but neither of them said anything to us. When I walked by, Nate stared at my hotdog and puffed out his cheeks. Allen and I were having such a good time, we just ignored him. We got back to our seats just when they were announcing who won the float contest. The freshmen came in last, big surprise, but I think we were the most entertaining. The junior float won, which made the seniors mad, but I bet they lost because they terrorized our cheerleaders and astronaut.

I did see my sister sitting down front with all the cool kids. She was pretty sure Asha was going to win, and started chanting Asha's name along with the rest of her crowd. When they announced Halle Murphy as the winner, Asha was the last one in the court to congratulate her. Figures. She's such a stuck-up Paris Hilton wannabe. I know I shouldn't be this way, but next time Asha is over to our house and says something mean, I will ask her how the homecoming vote went. She says mean things to me all the time, but I'll probably chicken out. I know how it feels to have your feelings hurt.

You know what, Mrs. Pope, it's funny how the "accepted" kids expect me to put up with their comments, but they can't take it when someone says something smart ass to them. Just for a day, I would like Asha or Nate to be me. Then they'd know what it feels like. Fat chance of that happening.

At the end of the game, Allen texted his dad to come pick us up. While we were going to the steps out of the stadium, the football team was walking off the field so everyone stopped to cheer for them. They went through the crowd on their way to the locker room. Most of them were real dirty and sweaty, but some were clean and I knew they didn't get to play. One of the guys who bothers me in PE was a clean one. He saw me standing there cheering for the team. He kind of nodded at me and then he stuck out his hand for me to high five. I hesitated at first, thinking he might pull his hand away. He didn't.

I think I will go to another game this year. Maybe my dad will go too.

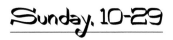

Sunday, 10-29

Paul spent the night again Saturday. He's all bummed because the boyfriend confessed to the murder. The kid said when they were having sex, he pressed too hard on Kimberly's throat. She started yelling at him about it, but he kept on doing it, and then he ran off and left her in the woods. He didn't think he killed her though. Paul still doesn't believe the boyfriend did it—the cops haven't released his name, even though they could because he's eighteen. Whether the kid did it or not it doesn't matter; he's already incriminated himself, and he's busted on account of statutory rape. Paul spent all night on the Internet and figured out the street Kimberly lived on and found a sexual predator who lived a few streets over from her house. The guy had been arrested on counts of child pornography, which I guess means purchasing videos and stuff online. Really sick stuff. Paul wants to go over to his house and check out his brand of cigarettes. I asked Paul how he knows this guy smokes, and Paul said he can just tell by how bad his skin looks. I don't know how he can tell that from an Internet picture. Most of the sexual predators we've seen have really bad faces, but that doesn't mean they all smoke. Paul said if you're a predator, you smoke to relieve the nervousness of committing that kind of crime.

Anyway, Paul wants us to act like we're selling merchandise for band, and then ask for a cigarette. The cigarette butts we found near the murder site were Marlboros, which is a common enough brand. I see them around school all the time. But Paul thinks if the cigarettes match up, it's a start. I wish he'd drop the whole thing and start acting normal again. When we played Super Smash, his mind was barely there.

Monday, 10-30

We're having a Halloween party at church Wednesday night, so I'm not going out in my old neighborhood. It's getting too dangerous over there anyway. One of my old neighbors told my mom that there are gangs running around, and she doesn't think many kids are going out this year. Seems ironic that we had a murder near our "safe" neighborhood, but Mom said that was not normal.

Tuesday, 10-31

Happy Halloween! I hope your twins have fun. I bet little Josh won't let you dress him up as a Raggedy Andy doll after this year. Three's the age limit for all that cutesy stuff for guys. Junebug (no offense, but I hope that's a nickname) won't mind it though. But if she's anything like my sister, she'll want to get all dressed up and be Cinderella at the ball. Or a cat. Why is it that all girls like to dress up like cats? I was a hobo for at least four years, and then my mom got the bright idea that it would be fun to make my costumes. I'm kinda bummed I'm not going out this year. I miss all the candy. Mom bought extra bags of candy corn so I won't miss out too much. She also bought bags of Snickers, which are my favorites.

Wednesday, 11-1

Mom finished my costume in time, so I got to dress up for the party. Not many of the teenagers wore costumes, but I didn't care because the little kids really thought I was the dad from *The Incredibles*. It was hilarious. Paul showed up and didn't say much about the murder. He was almost his old self. He didn't dress up, but he ran around acting like a werewolf. Everyone was cracking up about it. I noticed he had a big bruise on his face, but I pretended I didn't see it. He probably fell off his bike or something. If he didn't, it's really none of my business anyway. He seemed happy enough though. Almost hyper. He told me later he had a girlfriend. That explained a lot. Like why he wasn't so obsessed about the murder. He said somebody called Social Services about his mother. He asked if I had told anyone about her. I shrugged and said I didn't say anything to anybody. Paul said things got worse for him afterwards. I didn't have a chance to ask him what he meant, because a bunch of little kids jumped all over us. Paul ran after them and tried to scare them. We were all laughing like crazy.

The highlight of the party for me was the food. A parent committee brought in candy apples and brownies and stuff, plus we all brought bags of candy to share. I know I'm too fat already, but everyone would have thought I was nuts if I didn't gorge myself with candy, like a normal kid. Once I started eating, it was like I couldn't stop. When I got home, my stomach really hurt. My mom asked if I had a good time, and I said, "No, I ate too much." She brought me something to settle my stomach, but it didn't help. Guess that's what Halloween is all about for kids, getting sick on tons of candy and then feeling miserable afterwards. Same thing used to happen to me on campouts in the Cub Scouts. I would eat so many roasted marshmallows and s'mores, I'd always end up feeling like I wanted to puke. One time it went the other way, and I was so embarrassed I almost quit the Scouts.

Friday, 11-3

Please Don't Read This Page

Nate is a total jerk. I don't know if you know him or not, but he is. I can usually ignore people like him, but he is nothing but a bully. That is all I am going to say about him. That makes me sound like Forrest Gump. I just hope you don't have him in any of your classes for your sake.

I am writing this in gym. We didn't have to dress out because there's a game tonight and the coaches are getting all the stuff ready. The football players are showing off for the cheerleaders in our class while the rest of us are doing homework or playing around. No one is paying attention to us. We could be planning an escape from prison and the coaches wouldn't notice. As long as we stay in our cage, everything is fine. I don't really know very many people in here, and some of the guys say things about me, so no one talks to me much. This week can't get over fast enough and neither can this class. Not yours but the one I am sitting in right now.

Since Spencer doesn't sit with Allen and me at lunch any more, Nate decided to resume his usual antics. He pulled the top of his pants down so his underwear and top of his crack showed, then he stuffed his book bag in his shirt and walked around the lunchroom. Allen and I ignored him until he grabbed a handful of chips from Allen's tray and started stuffing them in his face. Nate made mouth noises like an idiot and had the entire cafeteria cracking up. Allen started crying and finally ran out of the lunchroom. I told Nate he was a stupid moron and that only cowards make fun of other people. I didn't care what people thought of me, I had to say something. Then Nate grabbed my hand, like he was gay, and blinked at me. "Hey sweetheart," he said. "You sure have some great-looking boobies." Then he looked at his friends, sitting a couple of tables away. "Slim Jim is upset," he said while batting his eyes. Kids started laughing, which usually makes Nate worse, but then Spencer came over and told Nate to knock it off. "Leave those guys alone," he said. "They're not hurting anyone." Nate smirked and acted like he was going to smart mouth Spencer, but with Spencer standing there all cool, and the added fact that he is a starting player on the JV soccer team, Nate patted Spencer on the back, and said, "Okay, that's cool, man. I get what you're trying to say. Those guys aren't worth my time." Then Nate saluted Spencer and went back to his table. Spencer gave me a look that said, "Sorry, I tried." But I felt pretty good that Spencer had taken up for Allen and me. Other than my parents and a few friends at youth group, no one had ever done that before.

Monday, 11-5

Please Don't Read This Page

If it isn't one friend it's another. Now Allen doesn't want to go back to the cafeteria. Not because of Nate, but because someone told his parents that he ran out of there crying, and now they are really steamed. They went to the principal's office and demanded that he do something about the way kids act at lunch. The principal called an assembly over the whole issue and talked about treating one another with respect. It felt like the entire student body was watching Allen and me, sitting like two fat dweebs in the freshman section. It was about the most awful ordeal I have ever been through. At lunch, we sat alone, hardly speaking, feeling like outcasts, like the Untouchables we read about last year when we were studying the caste system in India. I went from Mr. Incredible to Mr. Untouchable pretty fast. The entire school looks weird now, like a beige and gray prison haunted by sneering pod people.

Then, to make matters worse, the principal called our parents in, and now we all have to have a big meeting about the entire incident. I begged my parents not to get involved, but Spencer told his parents the kids were really mean to me too. "Why didn't you say anything?" my mom asked. I tried to tell her that ratting out the other kids would only make matters worse. That it's not as bad for me as it is for Allen. But they want to meet with the principal anyway. And they want to meet with Nate and his parents. I can't believe Spencer told his parents about the lunchroom disaster. Doesn't he realize he's made things worse? My life was hell before, and now it's going to be like living in ten hells. In math class, Nate whispered that I better not rat on him in the meeting. "Unless, you're a big kindergarten baby and need Mommy and Daddy to hold your dick for you," he sneered. Monday's the meeting, and my mom offered to drive Allen and me to school. Gee, golly, I feel lucky.

Maybe we'll move again this weekend.

Tuesday, 11-7

Please Don't Read This Page

We have a study hall in math today because Mr. L's sick, and the sub didn't know what else to do. I'm caught up on all my work except this journal, which goes on forever. So, now I'm working on English in math.

We had our big meeting this morning—I had to miss science class because of it—Nate glared at me when the office helper came to get me out of class. It was a long walk down the hall because I didn't know what to expect, but the meeting went much better than I thought it would.

Mr. Gardner asked what happened, and I explained about Nate (Spencer had already ratted on him) and how his making fun of us got all the kids around us laughing. Mr. Gardner wanted to know who the kids were, and I said it's a different group everyday, and that it would be too hard to single out anyone. Allen then piped up and said if Nate found out we told on him, he might beat the crap out of us. Allen said he wanted to forget about the whole thing, and I agreed.

Allen's dad said he wanted to have a meeting with Nate and his parents. Allen and I tried to convince him it would be the biggest mistake in the world to do that. My dad said we need to learn how to deal with Nate, because the world is full of Nates.

Mr. Gardner is a pretty cool guy, and he said that he understood how we felt, because he was a fat kid in high school. He's still pretty heavy, but no one wanted to point out the obvious. Besides, it's not as bad for adults, especially principals. I know it's a stereotype, but I bet there are more fat principals than skinny ones. Let's face it, kids are more accepting of heavy adults than heavy kids. Half the parents at our school are overweight, but you don't really notice. With kids it's different—there aren't as many of us, though Mr. Gardner said that's starting to change, which isn't a good thing.

Allen's parents said they thought the teachers should do a better job monitoring the students' behavior, and that Allen and I shouldn't have to worry about being picked on all the time. Mr. Gardner agreed. He said he's really been on the teachers' cases about watching for kids harassing others. He thinks he sees an improvement and hasn't had any real complaints until this incident. (I wanted to bring up Mr. L and how Nate gets away with murder in his class, but didn't think it would change anything.) Mr. Gardner said he's going to put more teachers on cafeteria duty now that's he's aware of the problem. I wanted to point out that more teachers wouldn't help that much, because most of them just stand around talking to one another, rather than watching the kids. Unless you have teachers sitting on lifeguard stands and carrying paintball guns, kids are going to get away with stuff.

My dad must have read my mind, because he said putting more teachers in the cafeteria doesn't really fix the problem. He said moral issues, like how to treat one another, should be discussed more often. My dad suggested teachers discuss some of these issues in homeroom. That way kids could talk about things like bullying and low self-esteem, and then maybe kids would get a glimpse of how the picked-on kids feel.

Mr. Gardner said he thought my dad's ideas were all good ones, but because it's a public school, the law won't allow that kind of teaching. It's too much like religion and there isn't time with all that the teachers have to cover. My dad shook his head, and said, "That's ridiculous. I'm not talking about teaching religion, but simple respect for humanity. Since when is the Golden Rule religion?"

Mr. Gardner again agreed with my dad, but said any teaching outside the curriculum would get a teacher fired, so most teachers stick with what is safe. I thought about some of the things you say in class, and they definitely are not safe. Like what you said about Pap and how he picks on Huck Finn. He bullies Huck because he's insecure about himself. That made me see Nate in a whole new light. I think he picks on people because he wants to look cool in front of the girls. If he thought he was already cool, he wouldn't need to show off to prove it. That's what's neat about literature—it deals with real-life issues, and we're allowed to discuss them because it's "in the curriculum." Allen's mom wanted to come and sit at our table with us, but Allen told her, "NO WAY!" I mean, how embarrassing would that be? Doesn't she remember what it was like being in high school? It couldn't have been that long ago. Just because we're freshmen doesn't mean we should be treated like elementary kids. Even my parents thought that was too much.

At the end of the meeting, Mr. Gardner said he would stand around in our lunch period for a while, to make sure things didn't get out of hand. He must have seen my reaction, because he said he wouldn't make it obvious why he was in there. I thought that was pretty cool of him, even though I don't think Allen and I need protecting. But at least our parents feel better about the whole thing. And I know that for the next month I'll be answering the question, "How was lunch today, Jimmy?"

Please Don't Read This Page

It's been two days since the meeting and nothing much has changed in the lunchroom. Mr. Gardner walked in for a minute, but he didn't stay like he said he would. I didn't even notice any new teachers on duty—the same two were still there, standing near the lady that sells cookies. The only thing that helped was that Spencer came by and talked to Allen and me for a couple of minutes, then went over and sat with some other soccer players. But I think Nate got the point.

My parents asked me if Mr. Gardner came around like he said he would, and I just said yes, because I didn't want to get them all upset and then call Allen's parents. With kids and their problems, things usually work out—it's just a matter of time. Most parents are too impatient to understand that.

People act like it's my fault that I'm fat, and maybe it is, but I don't eat any more than most teenagers. I just have a slower metabolism than a lot of kids my age, which means I have to work at it more. But no one told me this when I started putting on the weight. I mean, I didn't get like this on purpose. I was only a kid when this weight thing all started—I didn't know my eating habits made me this way until it was too late.

I don't get Mr. Gardner. Like, why didn't he show up in the lunchroom and hang around like he said he would? It's like he really didn't think it was that big of a deal. Like jocks picking on fat kids is normal. I bet he'd really freak if I started calling kids "dummies" because they don't get good grades like I do. I'd probably get ISS if I did that.

I mean, I have an uncle who died because he smoked when

he was in the army and got cancer. What if when my parents and I went to visit him in the hospital, we didn't tell him we loved him. What if we yelled at him for smoking. It was his fault after all. Or, what if I laughed at the kids who crashed in that wreck last month. They had been drinking, so, it was their fault that they almost died. No one would dare say anything mean to them, because they almost experienced a tragedy. But no one understands how much of a tragedy it is for a kid to be overweight, especially a kid everyone makes fun of.

Aren't my feelings important? Sometimes I sit in class and wonder if anyone would notice if I were gone. I guess Allen would, and Spencer. Maybe Nate, in a bad way. That probably isn't what a kid my age should be thinking about, but I can't help it. Thinking that way makes me depressed and then I eat more, which causes me to gain more weight, which causes more depression, and on and on. It really sucks.

Last week we watched *A Tale of Two Cities* in history class. The first line of the movie was "It was the best of times and it was the worst of times." At least I have half of that covered.

I don't mean to sound like I have the worst life, because I'm luckier than some kids. At least when I survive the bus ride home, I can be with my parents, my dog, and my video games. And church is great. People there accept me, all of me. And, I know that God sees inside my heart and knows how I treat others. Jesus was shunned by many people and he forgave them. I need to do that too. Last week at church, our pastor said that there are two ways to deal with life. We can see it as a problem or as a challenge. I'm not sure that there is much of a difference between a problem and a challenge, but I get the feeling that accepting life as a challenge is the better of the two. I'm not exactly sure why, because I like working out problems, like in math. But, I guess problems in life are more about self-esteem and relationships and stuff like that, which is harder, because there are lots of right answers. Talk about a multiple-choice test. Besides, problems never go away until you answer them.

Monday, 11-13

This weekend my family went to the mall. All day on Saturday, which was okay, but after a while, it started to get boring. My mom and sister take so long to buy anything, especially clothes. In this one teen store, I thought my sister would try on everything. The lady was getting sick of her, and me and Dad couldn't take it any more either. We left and told them we'd meet them at the Discovery Channel store in an hour. When we went back to find them, they were still in that same store! Then we went to Macy's and I decided to look around the guy's department for a cool sweatshirt. My mom went with my sister to Juniors and my dad wanted to check out the watches. I didn't find anything I liked, so I went to Juniors to look for my sister, and noticed these two cute girls walking down the aisle. I smiled at them, and they started giggling. One of them said, "If I thought he was hot, I'd be gay."

I tried not to let their words bother me, but they did. By the time I found the rest of my family, I was in a really bad mood. Mom suggested we go to the food court and have a snack, and that cheered me up some. They have a Chinese buffet place there that is so good. I got a box of Mongolian beef and two egg rolls. Then we got ice cream at the little corner store. It's the one where they're always standing there giving out samples. (Sometimes I walk by and get a spoonful, and then come back later, and it's a different guy, so I get another sample.) If you're ever in the mall, get the banana ice cream. It's great.

We went to the dollar movies to see *Spiderman 2*. It was pretty good but I liked the first one better. That's usually how it works with sequels. The monster guy was scary though. When he came crashing into the restaurant and threw the car through the window, that was pretty cool. I'd like to do special effects for the movies. That way, you get to have things end up the way you want.

On Sunday, we went to church and then I came home and did homework. Paul called to see if I could come over, but Mom put the brakes on that. This time Dad didn't take my side. So I hung out on the sofa and watched some TV. Dad played a few video games with me, and we ordered pizza and watched some of the Bengals game. Those guys are really big and no one bothers them. I would love to be strong like them; it would help me so much with things. I did talk to Paul, and he wanted me to sneak out of the house.

"That's just about impossible, you should know that. Besides, I'm under heavy duty watch. Mom still suspects I had something to do with the MySpace picture."

"Is Jessica still freaking out?" Paul asked.

"Things have kinda cooled with her. I think it's made her more popular. Mary Magdalene turned saint. And she's really eating it up too."

"Mary who?"

"Haven't you heard of *The Da Vinci Code*?"

"Isn't that what they used to save the *Titanic*?"

"I don't think the *Titanic* was saved. Never mind."

"Jimmy?"

"Huh?"

"Do you ever wonder what Kimberly felt while she was being murdered? Do you think she thought she would get away, or do you think she knew she was going to die?"

I thought about it for a second. "I don't know, man. She probably thought she would get away. At least hoped she would."

"I can't stop thinking about her. And the boyfriend. I know he's innocent."

"You need to chill, man. Let the police worry about it."

"The police don't know anything. They nailed the wrong guy."

"There's nothing you can do. We already got burned once. Next time we might get caught."

"So are you telling me you're out?"

"I think we need to take a break, is all."

"Just wait, Jimmy. When I catch the right guy, you're going to be sorry you weren't there with me."

"I'll help when I can."

"I knew you wanted in."

Geesh.

Tuesday, 11-14

Yesterday I had so much homework I barely had time to eat supper. It was insane how much I had. A ton of it in every class not to mention the paper you assigned us to write. It took me four hours to finish! I hope you're happy that it caused me to have no life. At least I got it done and today is not so bad.

I usually like writing persuasive essays, except for the

research part. There was tons of stuff on the Internet about global warming to support my side, so that was cool. Now that I'm done, I don't know how anyone could doubt that we're killing the ozone layer. I mean, I like technology and computers and stuff as much as the next guy, but I'd rather live like they did in the old days, like in the fifties and sixties, when there weren't so many mega cars and chemical waste eating up the environment. I worry about what the earth's going to be like when I'm as old as my parents. I feel sorry for people from primitive countries who have to pay for industrial countries' mistakes. Doesn't seem fair.

Which brings up another point. Why is it that teachers seem to pile on the homework all at the same time? Shouldn't there be some sort of a system, where teachers can check and see what projects other teachers are assigning during a certain time? Like if a research paper is due in English on one weekend, then the science teacher could wait until the next weekend to assign his big project. Then maybe kids wouldn't resent their teachers so much.

Hopefully, that won't happen again for a while—where I get so much in each class on the same night. Not that I mind doing homework but when it's that much, I despise every minute of it. I ate two big bags of Doritos tonight while I did my homework, so now my stomach hurts. I hate myself for eating so much. This isn't an excuse, but I couldn't stop myself. Whenever I stress out, all I want to do is eat. Seems like I'm stressed out all the time. Would serve my teachers right if I puked all over my homework.

Wednesday, 11-15

Please Don't Read This Page

After school today I rode my bike over to Paul's. His mother was already passed out on the couch when I got there. She has a major drinking problem. Paul showed me all the empty gin bottles in the garage. "She's like this most days. My dad tried to get her to go to AA, but that just made her worse."

I couldn't imagine her much worse than she was. Her lipstick was all smeared and her hair was dry and ratty. I don't know where Paul's dad was. Maybe out looking for a job. Or a new wife.

"Why don't you take a picture," Paul said. "Haven't you ever seen a drunk before? C'mon, we've got things to do."

We rode our bikes for almost an hour before Paul stopped in front of a gray house with a shed out back. "This is it," Paul said.

"Are you sure it's the right one? The grass is all cut and everything." It seemed too nice to belong to a creepy predator.

"You knock on the door and talk to him. See what you can find out."

"Why me? You're the one who found him."

"Because, well, because you might bring back memories of Kimberly, because you're, you know, kinda heavy."

"That's just great. I'll remind him of Kimberly, the girl he— KILLED."

"You don't have to yell in my ear. Don't worry, I'll be watching. If he drags you in, I'll call the police. Give me your cell phone, just in case."

"I thought we were going to act like we're selling things for band. We don't have anything to sell."

"We can do that next time. Just talk to the guy."

"Next time? There might not be a next time. Talk about what?"

"Ask him for a cigarette."

"Like he's going to give me a cigarette."

"He will if he thinks you're cute. Hurry up, Jimmy, we don't have that much time."

I was too angry to be scared, so I stormed down the driveway and walked right up to the front door and pushed the doorbell. I pushed and pushed, but no one answered. A striped cat watched me from the front window, acting like she was bored. But no other sign of life. I hustled back up the driveway.

"Guess he's at work," I said, getting on my bike.

"Or out killing someone," Paul added.

By the time we got back to Paul's house, it was starting to get dark, and there were lights on in Paul's house. I could see his mom walking around, so I guess she recovered. "I gotta go," I said.

"Maybe we can catch him home on a Saturday," Paul said hopefully.

"Oh, I really look forward to that. And what's this "we" stuff? I'm the one getting killed, not you."

"Stop whining, Jimmy."

Thursday, 11-16

I asked Spencer if he wanted to come over to my house and play Wii this weekend, but he couldn't because of soccer practice. And his relatives are in town, since next week's Thanksgiving and everything. But he said he would once soccer was over. He has practice everyday after school, especially now that they are in the finals, so we talk mostly on the way to school. He started taking the bus because his mother can't drive him any more now that she has a new job. We joke around some, and since he has lots of girlfriends, I told him about the girl in my science and math classes I really like. He knows her really well, and told me not to bother with her because she's uncool. She seems nice to me, and she's one of the prettiest girls in our school. She has long blond hair and a hot body. I feel funny writing that to my English teacher, but that's what Allen says about the really cute girls. Even my sister. He says she has a great rack and that makes me want to puke. He also says my sister's a fox and can't believe we're related. He says he wants to spend the night at my house just so he can talk to her. He has a plan about how I'll pretend to have to go somewhere for an hour so he can be alone with her. Like she would even talk to him. She's a junior and hates freshmen.

You asked me to write more about my sister, so here goes. She's weird! She spends way too much time worrying about what to wear. She's not into cool things like video games. My mom tried to get her to play an instrument, but she wouldn't have any part of it. She's kind of rebellious and really sensitive. She hates it whenever I play my saxophone. (I practice thirty minutes a day). When I practice, she yells, "Shut up, you freak! You sound like a mule in heat!" My mom gets mad at her, and then they fight. I don't know why she's so mad at my parents all the time. They want her to get good grades and stop being selfish. Which she is, big time, I mean huge! She doesn't go out of her way for anybody. My dad calls her a princess, but I think she is a spoiled brat. I call her Princess Loser. She thinks she is better than me because she's skinny. But I get straight A's, and I'm in the jazz band.

Friday, 11-17

PE is still loads of fun. We walk around the track for an hour and then go shower. Wow.

Saturday's the big game between Hanover and Taylor. I might go. Mom and Dad keep asking if I'm going. I want to but who knows. Since we've won a few games, all the guys are pretty cool in P.E. now.

I have band practice every day after school, so Allen now has to sit by himself on the bus ride home. He text messages me when he gets picked on, which is all the time. I tell him to ignore what those idiots say; he's better than they are.

I won't be in class Monday because I have a doctor's appointment. It's a little late in the year, but this is the only time they could get me in for my yearly check-up. My mom said Dr. Weber's office gives the kids playing sports priority over the rest of us, because they can't play without a physical.

Tuesday, 11-21

Please Don't Read this Page

The doctor freaked at how much weight I've gained. He showed me where I was on the chart and I was way up there. Dr. Weber took blood tests and made me pee in a plastic cup, just in case I have a medical problem. He said maybe it was my thyroid, but he didn't think it was that. He wanted to know if I was depressed. Or stressed. I said I wasn't. But I am. Who wouldn't be? I bet all fat people are depressed. Even jolly old Saint Nick. Being fat isn't so jolly.

Sometimes I look at myself in the mirror and think of Humpty Dumpty. I'm worse than that. I'm not even oval enough for an egg. Why do I eat so much? At church last week, there was a tray of donuts out. I ate five at first—then, I kept sneaking more. I almost made myself sick, but still kept eating. I've always loved to eat, mainly bread and chips and stuff, but I thought I was just being a kid. All my friends eat as much as I do, some even eat more, and they're not fat. When I was little, my parents told everyone what a good eater I was. Guess I was too good of one.

Dr. Weber said my risk is high for developing diabetes, and if I don't lose weight now, I'll be obese for the rest of my life. For the rest of my life? I can barely look at myself in the mirror now and I'm still a kid. What will it be like when I'm old, like thirty? This really sucks. How am I going to lose weight now? It's almost Thanksgiving break. I mean, isn't that what Thanksgiving is all about? Eating? My parents and relatives will be cooking all my favorite recipes, food that we don't have any other time, and I'm supposed to cut back? Life is so unfair. I wish I wasn't so fat. At least I don't look like a skinned cat, like Jessica.

Can my life get any worse? After math class today, I overheard Kaitlin Lewis talking about me in the hall. She was telling her girlfriends how she saw my crack last week when I leaned down to get something out of my locker. "He can't keep his pants up, he's so fat," she said. "I bet he keeps his pencils in there!" I had to go past them to get to my locker, but I was so humiliated, I went the other way, and then got in trouble for not bringing my book to Spanish. I just don't care anymore. I mean, what's the use? I've been kidding myself, thinking the kids look at me differently from Allen. I thought I was somehow better than him, not as fat—not by much, but at least a notch better anyway. But the truth is I'm not any different from Allen. We're two fat boys with cracks that show. Two pigs in a poke, my grandmother would say. I wonder how many times kids play "basketball" behind my back.

Some days the picking gets so bad, I feel like killing myself. I mean, I don't really see my life getting any better. Even the kids at youth group are acting all weird, like they have to be nice to me because we're at church, but none of them ever call me to do anything. Except for Paul. He's still cool. But for how long? At least I have my parents. But what if something happens to them?

I thought of different ways to kill myself, but even that's hard because of my weight. Hanging wouldn't work: because I'm so fat, the rope wouldn't hold. If I jumped out my bedroom window, I'd probably just break something because my weight would be too much of a cushion. I don't know where to get drugs, so dying of an overdose is out of the question, and we don't keep guns in the house. Until I think of a better idea, guess I'll just kill myself by overeating. Unfortunately, that takes years.

In case you really do read the pages, I'm not really serious about killing myself. I wish somebody else would kill me though. I don't mean that either. I wish I could be me, but in a different body. I was so depressed today that I asked if we could go to McDonald's. My mother bought me two Big Macs and fries. Why does she do that? Doesn't she realize that I'm fat? And eating junk only makes me fatter? She can be so clueless sometimes. I think she feels sorry for me, so she lets me eat whatever I want. She's overweight herself, so I guess she's not surprised I am.

Thursday, 11-23

Hi Mrs. Pope! Hope you're having a good Thanksgiving in Indiana. I bet your kids are glad to see their grandparents. Did you sing "Over the River and Through the Woods?" My parents used to sing that to Jessica and me on our way to Nana Josie's house when we were little. Another one of our family traditions.

I know you said we didn't have to write in our journals over Thanksgiving break, but I can't get to sleep and I don't feel like reading. I'm at the beach—we left yesterday, right after school was out and picked up Nana in Kentucky. Then Dad drove all night while we slept in the back when Nana wasn't snoring. My parents won't let me bring my Wii or PlayStation on family trips. We've been going to the beach over Thanksgiving for the last few years. We always go to the same place—Bald Head Island in North Carolina. Cars aren't allowed on the island, so we have to take a ferry over and then carry all our stuff on golf carts. Which is a pain, because we have big coolers filled with food and drinks, not to mention the turkey.

Anyway, my parents, along with my Aunt Sue and Uncle Jim, always rent the same house, a big gray one with porches all around. It sits right on the ocean, on the East Beach, and my parents always get my sister and me out of bed to see the sunrise. My aunt and uncle let my cousins Sophie and Audrey sleep in. It's not fair that we have to get up so early on our break, but once I'm up, I'm glad. Jessica usually goes back to bed afterward, but I go out and search for shells and fossils. The water's pretty rough on the beach, so most of the shells are broken, but they're still cool.

My twin cousins are in the fifth grade, and they can get

really annoying. All they want to do is play Monopoly and Sorry! and other really old games. I end up playing, but those games take forever. And if that isn't boring enough, my dad always buys these ridiculous jigsaw puzzles with a thousand little pieces and says we have to put it together by the end of the trip. Yeah, right, Dad. We've never put one of them completely together, so we just end up leaving it at the house for the next group of suckers to try. All our old puzzles are still at the house, so I don't know why my dad keeps buying more. My parents can be real old-fashioned sometimes. It drives me and Jessica crazy.

My aunt and uncle are really cool though. My sister says they really "get" teenagers. That's probably because they're younger. My aunt is my mom's younger sister and she's a social worker. She's always telling stories about abused and neglected kids and how hard it is to get help for them. I don't know if I could do her job; it sounds really stressful. She says she stays awake at night, because she can't get some kid's sad eyes out of her mind. Every second there's some kid out there hurting. It's her job to try to find that kid so she can get him help. It's mind-boggling to think about. My uncle is the opposite of my aunt—he's a sales guy for a drug company and he's always telling jokes. I don't know if I've ever seen him in a bad mood. I hope it doesn't have anything to do with him selling drugs.

The beach is okay, but it can be kind of boring. Except for Thanksgiving dinner—that's the highlight of the trip. People who own the house have a deep fryer, and that's how we do the turkey. It's the best. The aroma from the turkey makes me forget I have any stress in my life.

Sunday, 11-26

We had our usual Thanksgiving. Dad did the turkey, and my Mom made sweet potatoes with marshmallows, green beans, cranberry sauce, corn pudding, oyster dressing, and rolls right out of the oven. Nana (Mom's mom) fixed cornbread dressing and her famous lumpy mashed potatoes. She has a hard time getting around because she's so big. The whole ride to the beach, all she talked about was how her ankles were swelled up. Mom always gets pies from Frisch's—she usually only gets pumpkin, but this year she got pumpkin and banana cream. My sister got stuck snipping the green beans while Aunte Sue and the guys watched football. "That's not fair," she whined, like she's does every year. "Why do Dad and Jimmy always get out of everything?"

"Shut up, woman," I yelled from the family room. "You should know your place by now." Dad laughed, but Mom reminded her of how the guys get stuck with all the yard clean-up.

Nana tried to make Jessica feel better by saying we should be put on clean-up duty, but she didn't really mean it, because she said, "If they cleaned up, they'd make an even bigger mess." That's not true, since Dad and I do the dishes at least three times a week, but I wasn't going to disagree with Nana. It was too much fun watching my sister get all mad.

Nana is old school and doesn't think men belong in the kitchen. Mom said it's not worth arguing with her, so when she's there, Dad and I sit around doing nothing so we can "keep the peace." That's what my mom calls it anyway.

Wednesday, 11-29

Finally! Something fun to do in school. We got assigned a project in science class. We have to build a car out of a mousetrap. Next week we'll have a contest to see whose will go the farthest. The teacher gave us some hints on what to do and what not to, and I went online to find some other info. I'll work on mine this weekend. I'm sure Dad will want to help but he's not supposed to get over-involved. I really like it when me and my dad work on things together.

Nate is still a jerk.

Sunday, 12-3

Dad and I worked on my rocket mousetrap car yesterday and it looks great. It's all red and black and it goes a long way. I tried it in the driveway and almost lost it on its trial run because as soon as I let the spring go, my dog got all excited and chased after it. He was going to chew it up but I yelled at him and he dropped it. I had to get all the dog slobber off before I could test it again. It works great and I can't wait to see how it does against everyone else's in class.

In a little bit we're going to church. We went out to eat this morning at Frisch's; they have a buffet breakfast bar. Boy, is it good. I had French toast and biscuits and gravy. Then two big plates of eggs and some cereal. I hope I don't burp in church. One time, a few years back, I got hiccups in church really bad. It was a day when the preacher was very serious. I don't really remember what he was talking about, but no one else was making any noise. Right in the middle of one of his pauses, I let out this big hiccup. Everyone turned and looked at me. Even the preacher looked.

Mom turned red but I couldn't help it. The preacher went back to his sermon, but he kept looking at me, more than he ever did before. Every time he took a deep breath, he would glance over. Then, as if we had planned it, he paused again and right when he raised his arms to make a point, I let out another one. Except this one sounded like a small dog barking. The preacher dropped his arms and kinda laughed. Then most everyone else did too. Mom made me get up and we went out into the lobby. I'm surprised we ever went back to that church. Mom and Dad still ask me if I have the hiccups before we sit down in church. And so do other people. Mom laughs but she doesn't mean it.

Tuesday, 12-5

Today we got to see how our mousetrap car works in school. We went out in the hall and we each had our chance. When it was my turn, I was nervous but guess what? Mine went farther than all the others! It felt so cool to have the car that everyone else wanted. People who had never spoken to me asked me about it. Even Whitney said something, but I was so shocked I think I just turned red and mumbled a "thanks." A few of the guys were saying that you can attach some sort of rod to the spring on the trap, and it slows down the spring when it's released. I'm not sure what they mean but if I can figure it out, they said it will go even farther. So, we'll see this Friday when it really counts.

In lunch, some kid threw a chair across the room. It started when he got hit in the head with an orange. It was by accident—some kids were just trying to be funny and weren't aiming at him. But when he got hit, he went crazy and picked up a metal chair and just heaved it over three or four tables. It hit a junior in the head and then the whole room went nuts. Everybody was yelling and teachers came running. The kid got pulled away by the school cop. I don't know what happened to the kid who threw the orange, probably nothing, but the one that got hit by the chair had a big cut. There was blood all over the place so it ruined a lot of people's lunches. I thought the place would never calm down. Finally, the bell rang and we all wandered off to class.

Wednesday, 12-5

Please Don't Read This Page

I want out of gym class. I thought that maybe after a while the kids would stop bothering me but it's getting worse. Nate started everything again in the locker room, and then his buddies jumped in on the fun. I was putting on my PE shirt when he came over to me and grabbed the bottom of my shirt. He wouldn't let me pull it down. I told him to quit but he just laughed and said, "Hey guys, watch this, it's the Pillsbury Doughboy!" He poked me in the stomach and then did the little giggle like on the commercial. Everyone burst out laughing. He poked me pretty hard so I sat down and rubbed my belly. Nate patted my head. "Aww, does poor little Jimmy need a hug? Well, I would try but my arms aren't that long." And all the guys standing around laughed again. About that time, Coach walked in and asked what was going on. Nate stepped in front of me and said, "Nothing, sir. Just having fun before class." Coach looked at me but Nate had gone behind him and gave me a death stare, so I knew that if I told, he would harass me even more for ratting on him. Or he'd hit me. I just shrugged and told the teacher that I was fine, we were just playing. I don't think he believed me, and he yelled at everyone to get out in the gym where they belonged.

Every day I go to gym, I get nervous thinking about what they're going to do that day. Not all the kids bother me but those who don't just stand around and watch. They're probably glad I'm there so they don't get picked on. Just once I'd like for someone to stand up to Nate and his buddies. Maybe tonight in church, something good will happen. Youth group is usually fun. I hope Paul is there. High school is hard.

Friday, 12-8

Remember the mousetrap car contest? Well, today was the day that counted. As a grade. Everyone in the class had fixed their car so it would go faster and I thought I should too. But when I let the spring go, it just barely rolled. I got so flustered, I had no clue how to fix it. Whatever I tried didn't work and finally I had my last try. The wheels hardly turned; a turtle could've crawled faster. Nate said, "Nice going, Winterpock. Aren't they supposed to do better the second day?" A few people laughed but I pretended I didn't hear them. I couldn't look at Whitney but I knew what she was thinking. If I had done nothing to it, maybe I could have won. Oh well, at least I had fun the other day when it went a long way. This kid named Leo won.

Now we have to turn in our data and our teacher told us that we should learn from our mistakes. If that's the case, I should learn lots. What he meant was that our car should go farther the second time but mine didn't. I wish I could swap my days and then I would have been deemed the next Einstein.

Turtle car to rocket engine all in one day. I still haven't figured out what went wrong.

Youth group was fun on Wednesday night. I am so glad too because the rest of the week was not too enjoyable. Paul showed up and we played SSX Tricky on the GameCube at church. Then we played some more Foosball, but Sable didn't chase the ball under the table this time. I don't know what we're doing this weekend, so maybe Paul can come over. There is a playoff game tonight but I don't think I'll go. Allen isn't going so I don't know who I'd sit with anyway. I'd sit with Sable, but she might be with her other friends and they don't really talk to me much. I'll stay home and watch a movie or see how fast I can go through the levels of Super Smash Brothers.

Sunday, 12-10

Paul wasn't allowed to come over this weekend. He's grounded again; his parents wouldn't even let him go to church. He's in bigger trouble than ever because last week he snuck out of the house and took his parents' car. He drove over to the predator's house and knocked on his door. The predator answered the door, and Paul said he had a cigarette hanging out of his mouth. Paul swears it was a Marlboro. He told the guy he was on a committee to protect the parks in the area and asked the guy if he would sign this fake petition he had made up on his computer. Paul said the guy was real nice and signed right away. He even asked Paul if he wanted to come in for a Coke, but Paul freaked out and took off. When he got home, his parents were waiting for him. He said it was really ugly because his mother was drunk and his father was in one of his out-of-control rages. Paul hid out in the woods until his father calmed down. He said he felt safer in the woods where there was a murder than in the house with his father. I told him to let the whole murder thing go, but I know he won't listen to me. Guess I won't be seeing a whole lot of Paul.

Monday, 12-11

I saw another one of my sister's friends in the hall this morning. She is usually pretty nice to me, but when I raised my hand to wave she started talking to her friends. Maybe she didn't see me. As if that's possible. My bus was late this morning, so I had to walk into first period after class had started. Mr. Mackey stopped talking and waited for me to sit down. Then he said, "Well, Winterpock, thanks for dropping by." I told him our bus was late and just as he began to say something else, the announcement came on that Bus 34 just arrived. He kinda smirked at me and went back to giving notes on plate tectonics. I had to catch up.

Lunch today was so good. Turkey and dressing and mashed potatoes, and it's not even Christmas. And we had rolls. Soft and warm, they must be the one thing that all cafeteria people learn how to make. Our cooks are actually pretty good for a school cafeteria. Last year, our food was awful, but I would eat it anyway because I would be so hungry. The rolls would be hard and dry, like eating a piece of cardboard (not that I know what that tastes like but I can imagine). Everything would be brown – the rolls, the fried chicken, the corn, the lettuce, even chocolate milk.

You probably wonder if my mom still makes lunch for

me. She does but I save it for the ride home. My bus driver doesn't say anything to me about it; he's probably glad I'm not throwing things or cutting up. We have one kid that used to cuss at cars. One day, he yelled at the wrong car. The man driving it was an off-duty policeman and he called his buddies and they stopped the bus. This kid Jeremy was so scared. They made him get off the bus and tell them his phone number. The police called his mom and told her what Jeremy had done. I think he got in big trouble. He doesn't yell out the window anymore.

Wednesday, 12-13

On the bus this morning someone threw a paper wad at me and hit the back of my head. I didn't turn around because that just makes things worse. I looked at the driver in the mirror above his head—he glanced at me over his glasses and went back to driving. Then I got hit again. I still didn't move and someone, I think it was this kid named Ricky, said, "He's got so much cushion, he can't even feel it." I felt my neck turn red and I couldn't help it, but I spun around and yelled, "Yes, I can. Every time. All year I've felt it." They were shocked. When I faced front again, our bus driver was smiling. The guys in the back were quiet for one second and then they went back to being obnoxious. For the rest of that ride, at least, they left me alone.

Friday, 12-15

Allen's coming over tonight to hang out and have some cake and stuff. My mom's an awesome cook and makes the best chocolate cake. I invited Spencer over, but he was busy with soccer again. Paul's still grounded for taking the car out. I feel sorry for him. Even before the murder, his parents picked on him all the time for nothing. Half the time his mom is so out of it, she yells at him for what she imagines he said, and his dad just looks for stuff to yell at him about. And then they get all mad because Paul can't take it anymore and goes nuts and starts screaming back at them. It makes it worse that Paul's the only kid. Now that his father is out of work, he has nothing else to do but sit around and wait for Paul to mess up. Well, I hope his dad is happy now, because Paul finally did something really bad (stealing the car, hello!) for them to get all bent out of shape about.

Paul told me that when he was a little kid, he would try to get lost at the mall so that another family would find him and adopt him. But that just backfired on him because his dad would whip him for fooling around and not keeping up. My dad calls stuff like that a Catch-22. That's an Air Force term that means there's no way you can win, but you keep trying anyway.

Saturday, 12-16

Please Don't Read This Page

It stinks that Paul is grounded. Other than Allen, I don't have anyone to hang around with.

When I was little, it was easy to make friends. My parents would take my sister and me up to Lake Cowan in the summer, and after Mom spread the beach towels, I would run to the lake and jump in. My sister did the same thing. We both looked around for kids our own age, and in minutes we would both find someone to play with. My sister is two years older than me, so I wouldn't see her for the rest of the day. That was fine with me, because I found my own group of kids. We would play all day, and the new kids I met didn't care if I was chubby.

Mom always had a hard time getting me to come in for lunch. She enticed me with the promise of ice cream and candy, so I'd leave my buddies for the promise of sweets. It always worked.

When did it change? When did kids start caring about how fat I was? It wasn't until middle school, maybe 6th grade, that I noticed I was different from most kids my age. That's when the fat jokes started. Then Tommy Underwood pushed me down one day after school. I was waiting for the bus when he ran into me on purpose. I had a heavy backpack on and I lost my balance and fell over. "Humpty Dumpty had a big fall!" he hollered. "Four-eyed lard butt!" The other kids who saw me fall laughed, and Susan London said, "His hinny's so fat, he has to sit at a special desk." That wasn't exactly true. In some classes, I sat at a table with a regular chair instead of one with an attached desk, but there were some skinny kids who sat at the tables too. They were usually the slow kids or the ones with "emotional problems" or EPs, as some people called them. (Not me, though. I'm not THAT mean). By the time the bus showed up, all the kids were whispering and laughing. I wanted to tell on them but knew that would only make things worse. So, I quickly got on the bus and sat in the first seat and acted like I was really into studying my math book. The kids didn't say much to me on the bus, cause they didn't want to make Mrs.

Westby, our bus driver, mad.

My face got all scratched up from the fall, and my mom asked me about it when I got home. I lied and said that I fell during PE. I felt bad about lying to her, but she would get too upset if she knew how bad things were for me. She set out a plate of her homemade cinnamon buns and a glass of chocolate milk. The reason I remember that day is not because I was knocked down at the bus stop, but because my mom only let me have three buns. "Might spoil your dinner," she said when I reached for a fourth bun. I thought she was being mean, because she knew no matter how many buns I ate, I would always eat my dinner.

Sunday, 12-17

I told my mom I didn't want any more of her cinnamon buns. She uses butter in them, and that's really bad for you. I've been reading about obesity online, and found several sites that talk about weight loss. I printed out some of the pages and gave them to my mom. She was really surprised, and then she got all sad. As she read the pages, she looked up at me and her eyes started watering. She said she would help me lose the weight. She even said she was thinking about signing up for Weight Watcher's. She's overweight too, but it never seems to bother her that much. But I guess if you're heavy, it always bothers you. I tried to picture my mother skinny, like she was in her wedding pictures. She always jokes about how children equal weight. My mom said the first thing we need to do is get rid of all the junk food in the house.

We went through the pantry and took all the chips and

cookies and candy out and put them in a paper bag. "We'll give them to the church," she said.

I told her I thought we should throw them away. "Would you give a carton of cigarettes to the church? It's the same thing." She laughed and then crammed them in the garbage.

Monday, 12-18

Great news! Paul is coming to our school right after Christmas break. But it's bad news too, because Paul's parents lost their house. They couldn't make the mortgage payments, and now Paul and his parents have to move in with his uncle who lives in our school district. He said his parents are worse than ever and complain because they have to live in his uncle's basement, but they don't have any choice. Paul said the basement isn't even finished, except the floor is painted, and it's eerie sleeping there at night. His mother hung blankets up to separate the space into "rooms"; their kitchen is an old refrigerator and a microwave. His uncle gets all ticked off if they go upstairs too much. He's single and has girlfriends over all the time. My mom said I could invite Paul over anytime. Paul sounded weird when I talked to him, not the usual "my parents are screw-ups" weird, but like he was out there, not really listening, but not wanting to hang up. Paul is smart and a good student like me. You'll like him, if he gets in your class.

Tuesday, 12-19

Mom says if I really want to lose weight, I have to exercise. She wants me to walk with her in the mornings but there is no way. Instead, I'm going to run with Dad. We have to get up at 5:00, because he has to leave for work by 6:30 to avoid getting caught in traffic. Dad is in better shape than I am but he's had his share of cinnamon buns too. I asked for a Total Gym for Christmas. Dad said they're expensive, so maybe it could be a family gift. My sister thinks that's a waste of money, and we should do a family trip instead. She said it would take a lot more than the Total Gym for me to look normal, and I'm such a loser I wouldn't use it anyway. My mom heard her, and they got into another fight. My sister was born skinny and doesn't know how it feels to be fat. She stuffs her face with nachos and dip as soon as she gets home from school. At least she did, until Mom threw out the dip and chips. She also eats pizza all the time. But she never gains weight—my Nana says my sister's so skinny she must have swallowed a tapeworm. Nana Josie is from the old school and believes in wives' tales and superstitions. My mother told me that Nana used to cover all the mirrors in the house after a relative died. Nana also believes the devil takes another wife whenever it rains while the sun is still shining. Nana has always been fat, but now she is so big she can hardly walk. I love Nana, but I don't want to end up like her.

My mom joined Weight Watchers and said she's learning a lot about nutrition. She has to follow some sort of point system that she says is pretty easy to remember. There's a program for kids, but you have to get special permission from your doctor and go to meetings. I'd rather die than go to meetings, so I'm doing a modified version of my mom's plan. Mostly, I'm cutting out junk food and eating more fresh fruits and vegetables. Absolutely no soda, not even diet drinks, and desserts only on the weekend, and then only one portion. No donuts or fried foods at all. Mom insists, though, that I drink milk with all my meals. My stomach growls all the time now. Mom said that will go away once it starts shrinking.

Wednesday, 12-20

Sable's one of the best writers in our class. She writes poetry all the time and shares her poems in teen circle at church. They're really weird but make you think. She writes about how crazy and mixed up the world is. Sable has a thing about pollution. She thinks the air is really bad and doesn't like to go outside because she might get lung cancer. I think that's one of the reasons she wears long-sleeved shirts all the time—even when it's really hot out. Paul thinks she's bulimic because she smells like puke sometimes. I've never noticed anything.

Sable tries to talk to me sometimes after class, but I'm always in a hurry to get to PE. I don't get it—my parents say high school should be the best years of my life because of making friends and going to all the games and dances and stuff, but how do kids get to know one another at school when they're so busy rushing from one class to another? We don't even have time to use the toilet, we're so rushed. Lunch is no better. We have to scarf down our food in order to finish before the bell rings. Rushing only makes kids eat more, because there's no time for the hunger signals to turn off. After years of eating like this, scarfing becomes a way of life. No wonder some of us have weight problems. My parents get mad when I eat like that at home, but I still do it. My mom says high school kills good table manners.

Thursday, 12-21

Please Don't Read This Page

It's been pandemonium so far this week in science class. That's because Mr. M is having us dissect frogs. I mean, we should be singing Christmas carols or making funnel cakes or something, not cutting up frogs. Mr. M's doing what he calls pithing, where he takes a scalpel and cuts one of the frog's nerves, which leaves it brain dead. Then he attaches a battery to the dead frog and cuts it open so we can see the heart beating. No one's paying attention like they should because they're too excited about the break and presents and stuff.

The girls especially are acting clueless, and dropping things and messing up the frogs. Some of them screamed when Mr. M cut one open. He about had a coronary. He made us put everything away, and then he yelled at us for not listening. Whitney yelled back at him and said the whole thing was way too gross for her, and she was going to tell her parents to talk to the principal about it.

That's when Mr. M really lost it. He said, "Gross? You don't know beans about gross. Did it ever cross your mind that when you take a walk in the park or swim in the ocean, you're surrounded by feces? And semen? And pee? That a forest is one big toilet? Or an outdoor hotel for one night stands? That when you smell the insides of flowers, you're smelling their sexual parts? Where do you think the millions of creatures that inhabit the forests and oceans poop? In a Port-a-Potty? Do you think possums screw each other at the Super 8? And you think cutting up a little numbed frog is gross? Give me a freaking break!"

The entire class really quieted down after that. No one said a word, not even Whitney. I think everyone was shocked that Mr. M talked about sex in front of us. I think even Mr. M himself was a little shocked, because he didn't say much after that. Just something like "shut up and read your books." Then he mumbled about showing us a movie on Friday. I hope he doesn't get fired over it, because he's really a good teacher. Then again, he probably won't. No kid is going to rat out a teacher who talks about sex.

Friday, 12-22

I'm so glad Christmas break is finally here and finals are over. School's been really hard lately. Not the school work, but the kids. Most of the time, I do okay, but it's hard when no one ever asks you to do anything. It's like I don't exist as a real kid who's interested in things like other people. Most kids treat me like I'm one of those plastic punching dolls, the kind you punch over and over but they keep popping back up. Inside, I'm just like every other kid, but they don't take time to get to know me, or know that I listen to jazz and Christian rock, or that I like the Cleveland Browns. All they see are my great big blobs of fat. I'm trying to do something about it, but it's hard. I feel hungry half the night, then in the morning when I stand on the scale my weight's the same. My dad said our family's going to get a Total Gym for Christmas, and that way I can build some muscle. Dad says muscle burns calories faster than fat, so that should help.

I'm getting used to all the picking stuff, but that's not what's getting me—it's feeling invisible. I go hours at a time without anyone noticing I exist. That's worse than the picking. The teachers are just as bad. Except for you. I appreciate your putting us all in groups, rather than have us choose our own groups. I would never be chosen. Maybe Sable would choose me, because we're in the same youth group. She's always pretty nice to me in class. She's not as hot as Whitney, the girl from science, but she's pretty cute.

You'll be happy to know we talked about *A Separate Peace* at youth group last time. I really like the characters Finny and Gene and so does Sable. She thinks the book is about war and how people subconsciously fight wars everyday of their lives. That humans are conditioned to be warmongers, and that the big wars are a result of our everyday wars just piling up until they get so big, we're fighting country against country instead of person against person, or employee against employee, or company against company, etc. I think she has a point, but I think the story is about how some people hurt other people because they don't feel happy with themselves. I mean, look at Paul's dad. He's really unhappy because he can't find a job and is married to an alcoholic, so he takes his anger out on Paul, even though Paul is really a good kid. Gene feels inferior to Finny, so he shakes the branch and causes Finny to fall. Then Gene feels all sorry and guilty about it, but the thing is, he can't take it back, because Finny's leg is ruined for life. I think the author is trying to say that life is about humans going around hurting one another until they wise up and realize how bad they've been. Then they spend their lives feeling guilty about their behavior, and try to make it up by doing really nice things for the people they've hurt. I wonder if Paul's dad's going to make it up to Paul later on. It's hard to imagine. I suppose there must be some people who don't hurt other people, but I doubt it. My dad's really nice, but sometimes he says things that hurts my mom, and even my grandmother. I've said some nasty things to my sister—but I don't regret them, at least not yet.

Thursday, 12-28

Dad bought the family a Total Gym for Christmas—it's awesome. You can work every major muscle in your body. Dad's spotting me and I can lift around 90 pounds, so far. I've made a commitment to lose weight, first by cutting out all junk food and eating more bananas and apples and stuff like that. My mom says it's all about balanced meals—you don't have to starve yourself; you just have to get enough from each of the three food groups. You can pretty much eat anything you want as long as you have a balance of carbs and proteins, but limit your fats. She says I have to use common sense, like cutting out banana splits and jumbo-sized French fries. I really try to stay away from donuts and chips, because I know once I start eating them, I go too far. Remember all the donuts I used to eat at youth group? What was I thinking? The thought of all that sugar makes me want to puke.

I've committed to running a mile four days a week, and

working out on the Total Gym three days a week. This won't be as hard over Christmas break, but once school starts up, I'll have to get up at five in order to run and get my workout in. Mornings are so cold but it's the only time I have to work out because of school, band practice and homework. Plus, if I wait until after school, I'm usually too tired to get motivated. Dad said mornings are the best time to work out anyway, since it gets your metabolism going for the rest of the day. I've already lost three pounds since Mom and I threw out all the high-carb snacks. The scale isn't groaning as much as it used to. Things are looking up.

Monday, 1-1

Happy New Year, Mrs. Pope!

Hope you had a great Christmas break. Every Christmas Eve we have a special celebration where we go outside and sing carols around the manger. Then we prepare baskets of food with hams and turkeys to take to the soup kitchen on Christmas Day. This year my family woke up real early on Christmas Day, and we helped pass out the food baskets. People were really happy to get them. Some of the little kids looked really excited, which goes to show you how much we take for granted. There's always been plenty of food around my house, too much of it most of the time. Same for most people I know. I mean, I can see getting excited about a Wii or a Total Gym, but food is something that comes with the house. Or so I thought before this morning. It made me feel really bad to think that some kids don't get enough to eat and their moms can't afford to make their lunches.

When I stare at the fat on my body, I think of the poor kids who can't gorge themselves with cookies and rolls, and I feel really guilty. I told Dad how I felt and he said that sometimes a lot of weight doesn't mean you've eaten too much. It means you've eaten the wrong things. He said he sees many obese poor kids; he says it's because they can't afford to eat healthy. Places that offer free food can only afford to hand out the cheap high-carb foods, like white bread and boxes of macaroni. Sounds like another one of those Catch-22 things my dad always talks about.

Thursday, 14

Please Don't Read This Page

Paul came over yesterday and looked really weird. I didn't see him at all during Christmas break, not even at church. I caught my parents looking at each other when they saw him. He's let his hair grow out—it's below his chin—and it doesn't look like he's washed it in a week. He even dresses different now. And then he wears this stupid hat, a French beret thing, and his jeans are really big with chains hanging on them. Paul showed me his schedule, but we're not any of the same classes. He says school's a waste of time and all teachers are losers; otherwise, they'd be doctors or businessmen. I had to keep the windows in my room open and spray Lysol, because he smokes. My parents would freak if they found out he was smoking in my room. He said he smokes weed too, and that I should try it. He said I need to chill out and stop worrying about my weight so much. Paul has a real attitude. I think his parents are getting to him and he smokes pot to escape from them. He's got a new girlfriend and he talks about all the things they do together. Things I can't write about in here. What if you dropped the journal and it accidentally opened to this page? Not a chance I want to take.

Paul brought up the killer again. He and his new girlfriend have been spying on the predator's house at night. Paul's girlfriend's brother has a car, so he drives them over there, so they can watch in the windows. The man's always on the phone and drinking a beer. He paces around the house and sometimes sits in front of the TV. Not a very exciting life if you ask me. So far, no proof that this guy murdered Kimberly. Paul's thinking about calling the police about him anonymously. I think it's a long shot. Or a wild goose chase. But, so far, it's been a long goose chase.

I have to study for our test on *A Separate Peace*. Wish I could be more like Finny. I can identify with Gene Forester, because sometimes I get jealous of Spencer's life—I mean he can get any girl he wants, he's smart, he's a great athlete—how lucky can one guy get? Just like Finny.

Friday, 1-5

I'm pretty sure I aced the test today. Some of the kids were complaining because of so many long essay questions, but I'm glad you don't give those True/False tests. I think it's bogus to ask questions about what color shirt the kid wore, and picky stuff like that. It's better to ask what we got out of the book and what we think of the characters. I mean, you can't really answer questions like that if you haven't read the book. And it's a lot harder to cheat on essays tests. I do better on them anyway, probably because I like to write. I guess you're surprised at that, since I complained so much about writing this journal. But now I think it's pretty cool and it gives me a chance to record things that are happening in my life right now. I'll never be fifteen again or feel the same way as I do now. Like how much pressure my parents put me under. I mean, they're nice and everything, but they want me to be the perfect student, the perfect musician, and now they're pressuring me to try out for baseball. They keep bringing it up because when I was in the fifth and sixth grade, I was pretty good at it. Especially at pitching. I guess they forgot about the football and soccer disasters in the seventh and eighth grade.

No matter what I say, they just don't seem to understand. I told them I can't keep up with all my classes and play sports. Especially since they expect me to get all A's, and I'm involved with all my church activities. And I made Honors Jazz Band—seems like that should be enough.

Saturday, 1-5

My parents think I spend too much time alone in my room playing video games. I do that some but I spend a lot of time on homework. I'm reading *Lord of the Flies*, since you gave us four chapters to read over the weekend, which I think is unfair. Don't get me wrong, I like the book, but we do have other classes. Plus, you expect us to write in our journals on the weekends.

Okay, I just finished the chapters you gave us. They were pretty good, but I have one problem with it. Thanks, Ms. Pope, for picking a book that has a fat kid named Piggy on page five.

I hate all the description too. The best parts are when the book talks about the kids and how they form teams. Jack gets all the jocks, while Ralph gets stuck with Piggy, who can hardly see, much less run all over the island. The way the boys make fun of Piggy reminds me of last year when I was on the SAY team. We had practice on Tuesday afternoons, and this one day it was really hot—I mean like an oven. So everyone was really exhausted. Our coach decided about half way through practice that we were going to split into two groups and scrimmage. He had vests to put over our shirts to separate one team from the other, but since it was so hot out he decided to have us go skins and shirts. I really wanted to be on the shirts team because I'm so big and when I run, my chest flops up and down.

Well, you guessed it. I was put on the skins team. Once I heard that, I said, "Ummm, coach..." But he ignored me and said, "Come on, Winterpock." So instead of putting up a fight, I took my shirt off even though I knew I was going to be embarrassed. Right when I took my shirt off, I heard a snicker and knew I had made a big mistake. I ran to my position anyway, and as I ran, I looked at the ground so I wouldn't have to look in the eyes of any of my teammates. When I got to my position, I looked up and the team was staring at me with grins on their faces. The scrimmage started and it worsened. Since I was so big, I couldn't run that fast. It didn't matter which way I ran, I'd run and the kids near me would laugh, especially the one who I was trying to get the ball from. All practice kids laughed and pretended to be me by moving their hands up and down on their chests. When coach said practice was over, I ran to my shirt and put it on real fast. I then ran all the way to the car where Dad was waiting to pick me up. That was my last practice and the last time I played on a soccer team. I told Dad I hated soccer and I wanted to quit. But that was a lie. I really like soccer.

Wednesday, 1-10

Yay! We had a snow day today. By the time it quit snowing, we had five inches. It was so exciting to see our county's name at the bottom of the TV screen.

Since I was stuck at home, I watched TV all day. TV is full of food commercials. No wonder there's such a weight problem in our country. I'm not blaming my weight on TV, but it doesn't help when they keep throwing Big Macs and Whoppers with jumbo fries in your face all the time. It's all about making money for corporate America—who cares about all the health problems people, especially kids, have because of junk food? And then there are the cereal commercials with all the sugar, and candy bars, and those snack packs with hunks of fat in them, not to mention all the beer commercials. Now someone's come out with pre-packaged peanut butter and jelly sandwiches cut into cookie-shapes with the crust removed. I mean, how hard is it to make a peanut butter and jelly sandwich from scratch out of a couple jars, which probably has about half the preservatives of the prepackaged stuff? It never stops. Kids, especially little kids, want their parents to buy them what they see on TV. I know I did when I was little. I remember crying for Captain Crunch at the grocery store because I had seen it on television. You never see commercials for fruit and vegetables, only food filled with fat. I don't ever remember being anything but fat, but it never bothered me until now. My doctor said obesity can cause all kinds of health problems, and that bothers me. I'm trying to do something about my weight, but it's not coming off fast enough. I really work hard at not eating so much, but when I get on the scale I'm still fat, so then I don't try anymore. I wish there was a magic pill that could make all my fat go away. Then I'd have more friends and be really happy.

Sunday, 1-14

Lord of the Flies

I like the book, but kids from our class make oinking noises in the hall when they see me. Or yell, "Piggy! There's Piggy! Get his glasses!" It makes me sick inside when they do that. None of the teachers hear them, so they never get in trouble. The kid who sits behind me in math wrote "Piggy" in pen on the back of my good shirt. My mom was really mad about it and wanted to go to the principal. I begged her not to. It would only make things worse. I sent a note to Mr. L asking if I could move. He read it but didn't do anything.

You said Piggy was Jack's super ego because he always follows the rules, and he's a parent figure, unlike the rest of the boys who run wild. I guess I'm like Piggy, because I follow the rules, and do pretty much what my parents tell me to do. I really like my parents and don't see any reason trying to get away with stuff. I tell them everything, except how the kids at school tease me.

Paul can't tell his parents anything. It's worse now that Paul's into Kimberly's murder and stuff. He still comes over a lot—when he's not grounded—and sometimes he spends the whole weekend with me. It's more like he doesn't want to go home, rather than he wants to stay at my house. His parents stopped going to church, but Paul still goes sometimes. We pick him up on Sundays if he calls us in time. Most of the time he reeks of weed and alcohol, but my parents never say anything about it. I think he goes to church to get away from his parents. I feel sorry for him, sorrier than I feel for me. His dad rips on him about everything.

Last year he ran away from home and came to my house. He hid out in my room, but his dad figured out where he was. When Paul heard his dad's voice downstairs, he started shaking.

Then his dad yelled at him to come down. Paul tried to climb out the window but saw it was too far down and gave in. His dad called him a "stupid, idiot kid" and threatened to whip him. My dad tried to calm Mr. Grove down and told him that's not the way to solve problems.

Mr. Grove didn't listen and pushed Paul out the door. When they got in the car, I think his dad backhanded him. I felt so bad, and my mom started crying. My mom called Social Services, but they said it wasn't bad enough for them to do anything.

When the Groves found out my mom called Social Services, Paul wasn't allowed to talk to me on the phone for two weeks, and I didn't see him or his parents at church for a month. When he finally came back, he was the same old Paul, and I was glad to see that his dad didn't kill him or anything. We've been best friends ever since.

Paul came to church with us today, and he looked really bad—his eyes were all red and his hair looked like he had poured Crisco oil over it. He had on jeans with holes in the knees and a raggedy shirt. Not exactly church dress. But my parents acted like he was the most clean cut kid they ever saw and joked around with him and stuff. He laughed and told them some story about a kid who flunked his driving test six times, and seemed like the same old Paul again. After church my parents dropped us off at McDonalds and I told him how the kids at school call me "Piggy." I tried to make a joke out of it, but I really wanted him to tell me it's no big deal. Instead, he told me what happens to Piggy at the end of the book. He said it might give the mean kids ideas, and they might do the same to me. I don't really take him seriously, but I admit I'm a little scared. When I read the book now, I can't help but think I'm Piggy, I hear it so much. Lately, I've been getting a stomachache on the bus ride to school.

Monday, 1-15

Spencer's been acting funny lately. He never comes over and talks to Allen and me during lunch anymore. He doesn't even sit with us on the bus in the mornings, but I can't blame him for not wanting to hang out with a couple of fatties. Spencer's a popular kid and we just bring him down. The girls really like him. They're always going out of their way to talk to him.

That girl in my science class I really like, Whitney Elliot, the one Spencer doesn't like, volunteered to be my lab partner. I wrote up the reports for us—she had some good ideas. I mean, she's smart, but only one of us needed to write up the report, so I took up the slack. I did feel uncomfortable at first, like she was using me, but then she started talking about litmus tests and how she loves science and how she came in third in her 8th grade science fair, and how she really wants be a chemist someday, so I changed my attitude. Just because a girl is really pretty doesn't mean she's not smart. Whitney is saving up for a telescope, one of those really expensive ones. I told her about my dad's telescope and how we can see Jupiter through it. She loves to read Crichton books, and so do I. We both read *Jurassic Park*. We got along really good in lab, but she doesn't talk to me any other time. Probably because of my weight—I keep thinking what the doctor said. If I don't lose it now, I'll be fat all my life. I think he said obese instead of fat, but there isn't any difference. Fat is fat.

The speech we read today by Martin Luther King, Jr. was cool. He hoped that one day we wouldn't judge one another by outward appearance, but value people by how they are on the inside. My Nana always says "beauty is as beauty does." Old people say that a lot. I'm not old, but I agree with Nana and Dr. King.

Tuesday, 1-16

Paul rode home with me on the bus. Allen wasn't in school today, so the picking wasn't as bad as usual. Paul laughed back and shot the bird to everyone. The bus driver had to stop the bus to quiet everyone down. She told Paul that next time he needs a note from the office or he's not allowed on our bus. He started to smart off to her, but I told him it wasn't worth it. She'd kick him off the bus and he'd have to walk the rest of the way. I was glad when we finally got to my stop.

My mom ordered pizzas for us, two larges from La Rosa's. While we ate, Paul told me his dad lost another job. "It's really bad," he said. "Dad sleeps all day, and my mom's drinking's getting worse. She yells at him all the time and calls him a no good bum and lazy ass. He's been in bed almost two weeks. He only gets up to pee, and then two nights ago, he wet the bed. Can you dig it? A grown man wetting the bed. He won't even look at me anymore, and yells if I try to talk to him. Man, you don't know how good you have it."

I feel sorry for Paul because his parents are crazy. It seems so unfair that kids are at the mercy of their parents' character. Paul wouldn't have chosen an alcoholic mother or a mean father. I think if kids had a choice they would pick parents like mine. But even they're not perfect. As good as they are, they still let me get fat. For Paul, there's nothing I can do to help other than listen.

He hasn't mentioned the murder lately. I guess he has other things to worry about now, like living in his uncle's basement with his parents. At least he has his girlfriend but he thinks she's cheating on him. He found an empty sex wrapper in her car. You know, those things you buy at the drugstore that guys use so they don't get a girl pregnant. Anyway, she said she let her girlfriend use her car, and that the wrapper must have belonged to her friend. But Paul doesn't buy it. He says every time he calls her to "party," she makes up some kind of excuse. And she doesn't call him back right away, like she used to. Man, he's going to be really bummed if she breaks up with him.

Anyway, the news has calmed down about Kimberly. The only thing they say is that her boyfriend is on suicide watch. That really sucks.

Wednesday, 1-17

Ok, I don't get it. What a crazy story. A bunch of kids get stranded on an island. One kid picks up a conch shell, gets everybody together, and then gets voted the leader. But another kid gets jealous and turns half the kids against the leader kid, and they put on war paint and run around with spears and threaten to kill the kids who are just trying to build shelters and a fire. Why do kids give bullies so much power? Ralph was fair. He had a plan for survival and rescue, but Jack just wanted to hunt and kill. And he was really mean to Piggy. He even gets the kids to kill Piggy. I don't know if I agree with Golding—I think a bunch of kids would be so scared they'd follow any kid who acted like an adult. I know I would. Kids complain about their parents, but hate it when they have crappy ones, like Paul's parents, who half the time don't know he exists. Maybe that's what's wrong with Jack—he probably had parents like Paul's. Kids want to know that there's someone who'll stop their behavior when it gets out of control. The only thing that gets out of control with me is my eating.

My parents don't say much about my weight, because they can see I'm trying. They tell me all the time how proud they are of me. I get good grades and pretty much do what I'm supposed to. I don't sneak out, do drugs, smoke or drink, so they probably think they got off easy with me.

I know they compare me to my sister who's really moody and yells at them for nothing. They worry so much about her, I guess it's a relief that I'm not a pain like she is.

Thursday, 1-18

No offense, but what you did yesterday was useless. It didn't really prove anything, because the class knew that an adult would walk in any minute. Some of the kids ran around the room and threw things and someone, I'm not saying who, searched through your desk. A few morons wanted to skip out, but I warned them they'd get caught. I passed out the worksheets you left on your desk, and some of the class got into groups and tried to follow the directions. I got hit in the head with a pencil, but I mainly stayed to myself. The class could be described as controlled chaos. Everyone was out of their seats except for a few of us. I noticed even the loud kids kept checking the door to see if you were coming. No one pressed the call button, because we didn't want to get you in trouble for not showing up for class. That's because everybody likes you. If you were one of the disliked teachers, like Mr. Sammons, the class would have pushed the button.

Sable Moore said she thought you were one of the best teachers she's ever had, and couldn't believe you didn't show up for class. No one had a clue you did it on purpose. I don't think you got what you wanted. We didn't have any Jacks or Ralphs, but we did have a Piggy. That would be me. At least I didn't get killed.

Friday, 1-19

Please Don't Read This Page

Can't wait to finish this book. We've been on it forever. Now we've got to watch the movie. What's next, the play? You'd think the kids would learn something from the book, but it's only made them worse. After class, kids kept yelling at me, "Kill the Beast!" In lunch, a kid in our class yelled, "It's Piggy!"

and the girls at Whitney's table all laughed. Even Whitney. I thought she would have defended me, especially after our talks in science, but I guess she was too embarrassed to admit she likes me, even as a friend. But what did I expect? That some hot girl would ruin her reputation by hanging out with me?

I wish I could die. Why am I still fat? I know kids who eat nothing but junk food, and they never work out, and they're not fat. I looked up causes of obesity online, and one site talked about hydrogenated oils and trans fat, and how they weren't in foods until the 70s. Now they're in almost everything we eat, and that's why there's so much obesity. Same with high fructose corn syrup. It's a sugar that turns into fat as soon as it enters our bodies. And it's almost impossible to get rid of. But most people don't know about all the bad things they eat because of false advertising. It's not fair that food companies are making money on products that are so bad for us. There are warning labels on cigarettes, why not labels on foods? Warning: This product may cause obesity and get you picked on and laughed at.

Saturday, 1-20

I don't know why the class complains about grammar. It's easy. I mean, why kids can't see the difference between a subject and predicate is crazy. You explained it really good today, I mean, you really explained it *well*. It was cool when you said a verb is like the engine of a car, but half the class didn't listen. Some of the kids were mean about it. I don't know how you can take it. All they do is complain about too much homework, then ask you about extra credit. If they can't do their homework, how can they have time for extra credit? I can't stand kids who constantly complain about their grades and try to get you to change their test grades. I think I did pretty well on my *Lord of the Flies* essay—I really think Piggy is the superego and not Ralph—Ralph plays around and swims in the lagoon and does kid stuff, but Piggy never does. He always tries to take care of everybody and makes sure things are fair, even more than Ralph. Seems like at times Ralph is embarrassed by Piggy, and makes fun of him like some of Jack's tribe. Piggy gets his feelings hurt and can't understand why Ralph would want to hurt him, and then Ralph comes to his senses. Jack is definitely the id—he's all about his own pleasure and doesn't think about the good of the community. I've heard the human brain isn't fully developed until we're twenty-one. That explains why so many teenagers do such stupid things, like get into drugs and get pregnant and stuff. They don't know how to control their ids. I have automatic id-control: my fat body. I don't have many friends and hang out mainly with my parents and church group. It's hard to mess up under those circumstances.

I think Simon, not Piggy, understood the beast the most. Most of the kids thought it was a monster that they could kill and then get rid of forever. But Simon has this revelation that the beast is an invisible spirit with a life of its own. Kind of like those subliminal messages that are in television commercials. If we don't pay attention, it will leak out and become an obsession. It's like the obsession takes over and the person becomes somebody else. I watched an old movie once about some aliens called the pod people who came to earth and inhabited human bodies. The people acted weird, and their families were all worried. The beast's like an alien who comes and takes control of your mind. Sort of like what happens to Paul's mom when she drinks, or kids when they get high. If we don't control the beast, it will kill our souls. Like it did to Jack's tribe on the island.

Monday, 1-22

It was my fault Sable got in trouble with the substitute teacher. She got fed up with how rude the kids were to Mr. Connelly. I mean, he kind of asks for it and stuff. Kids nowadays don't really like listening to Andy Griffith CDs, especially when they're forced to. I bet at one time Mr. Connelly was a really good teacher, but not any more. He's too out of touch with teenagers today. The kids were really making fun of him and laughing too loud at the CD. At first Mr. Connelly thought they were on his side and laughing with him. Then he caught someone mimicking him, and you could tell his feelings were hurt. He got mad and turned off the CD and told us we were rotten kids and he wasn't going to teach us any more. That's when things got really bad, especially for me. Someone threw a note on my desk, and when I opened it, it said, "We wish you would fall off the mountain like Piggy." I put my head down on my desk so no one would know I was crying, and I could hear kids laughing. Sable came over and took the note from me. After she read it, she started yelling at the class, "You're the real pigs, you assholes!" The sub turned red in the face and said that he was going to write her up, which he did. Then he made Sable go to the principal's office.

Later, the principal called me to his office and asked about the note. I explained to him that the class doesn't normally act that bad, even for substitutes, but Mr. Connelly has a hard time with class management. You're probably wondering where I got that. Our next-door neighbor's a teacher and she talks about "class management" all the time. Anyway, Mr. Gardner seemed surprised about what I said. He asked if the kids treat me like that all the time. (Duh, hello! Remember the lunchroom incident?) But I didn't bring any of that up. I just told him when you're the fattest kid in the class, you expect to get picked on. I told him Sable was defending me and shouldn't get in trouble. He agreed and said the whole thing was no big deal, but if the kids start harassing me again to let him know.

"I don't understand what happened in there today, but it's very puzzling," he said as I was leaving. He sounded just like the Grinch, who "puzzled and puzzed till his puzzler was sore." It's not puzzling to me though. Guess he's forgotten how bad kids treat one another. Which is really strange when you consider that he's around kids almost every day of his life.

Tuesday, 1-23

I just found out that Sable got changed to my lunch period. Not that it makes a big difference in my lunchtime life. She never comes to the cafeteria anyway because she hates all the food. She says there's nothing edible in there because it's all loaded with animal fat and she's a vegetarian. A lot of kids skip lunch and just hang out in the halls. Man, I couldn't do that. By the time lunch rolls around, my stomach is killing me, I'm so hungry. But it's getting better lately. Ever since I've cut down on sugar and have been working out with my dad, my cravings aren't as bad. At first, the turkey sandwiches on wheat my mom packed for me weren't enough, so I would get a burrito or some fries in the lunch line. But when the scale continued to stay the same, I knew I had to cut out cafeteria food altogether. After a few days of eating an apple or pretzels with my sandwich, the cravings slowed down. But what really helped was when I got on the scale Sunday, and saw that I was down six more pounds, a total loss of eighteen pounds in three weeks. I even feel a little lighter, no kidding. My arms are getting some muscle to them too. Mom says I'll be solid as a rock if I keep dieting and exercising. My sister says I'll probably have a relapse and put it all on again. I've noticed she's not as skinny as she used to be, and I told her so. "You better cut down on the fries and Big Macs," I told her. "Pretty soon you'll be the chubby one and I'll have the hot bod." She went into another one of her tirades and shut herself in her room. Mom said I must have hit a nerve and to leave Jessica alone. Fine with me.

Thursday, 1-25

Sable started to wear black all the time, which makes her skin look paler than usual. She told me after class one day she hates her hair because it hangs in stringy, brown rattails. "I wish my hair was thick and dark like yours," she said. But my hair's a pain because it's so curly. That's why I keep it so short.

In our group last night Sable described herself as a "voracious" reader and an "ascetic" poet. Sable likes to use words that you have to look up in the dictionary.

Anyway, she told us she's worried about her younger brother, not now, but later, when he gets older. Jason's autistic, so her parents have to work with him all the time to do basic things. At least he can dress himself and go to the bathroom on his own, sort of. His parents made a sign for him and put it above the toilet so he can't miss it. The sign has two columns: Number One and Number Two. (Only they use other terms that I'm not going to use here.) Under each number his parents have written the steps Sable's brother needs to follow to complete his task. He decides which way he has to go, and then he follows the steps on the sign. Sable said if the sign wasn't there, her brother would forget to do basic things, like undo his zipper or take down his pants. Jason is already eight years old, and Sable worries about how he'll get by when he's an adult. His parents won't always be around to make signs for him. She plans on joining the Peace Corps after college and live in Zimbabwe, so she won't be around either. She started crying and everything, saying how hard it is on the family worrying about Jason all the time. He's so sweet and innocent, yet simple things are really tough for him. She hugs him every night before he goes to bed, but he just pushes her away and would rather hug his stuffed animals than Sable. At the mall he gets scared and screams at the top of his lungs, and everyone stares. Sable gets so mad because people yell at him and at her mom for letting him scream. Her mom can't do anything about it because he's autistic.

Our youth minister told Sable she needed to keep things in perspective and not lose herself in worrying about Jason. He said Sable needs to pitch in and help more, but she also needs to deal with her own life as a teenager. Our minister gave her some books to read and I bet she'll read them all because she's a "voracious" reader.

Saturday, 1-27

My sister and I used to be closer, but lately she has been acting strange, I mean stranger than usual. Every time I walk by her room, she's in front of the mirror staring at herself. She can't walk by a mirror without stopping and fixing her hair. She even primps in the car windows before she opens the door to get in. Then she complains all the time about how terrible she looks. I mean, if she thinks she looks so bad, why does she stare at herself every chance she gets? She complains to my mom about needing new clothes almost everyday—it's ridiculous. You should see her room—she has clothes all over the place. It's the biggest mess. My mom says if she picked up half the clothes on her floor, she'd have plenty to wear.

We used to tease and kid around a lot, but she doesn't want to do anything but talk on the phone and read her stupid magazines. At least she plays lacrosse and is pretty good at it. Mom says she's going through a phase, that all girls go through it. I asked Mom if she was moody like Jessica when she was a teenager. Mom laughed and said she was much worse. I can't imagine Mom moody; she's always so laid back.

Mom said it takes a few years for teenagers to get used to their raging hormones. The only hormones I feel are my hunger hormones. I'm hungry all the time, especially for pizza and Big Macs. Lately I've been craving Chipotle and the blooming onion at Outback. The blooming onion is really awesome. My mouth waters just thinking about it. But I don't give in half as much as I used to. Grandma says I'm the perfect dinner guest because I always ask for extra helpings. Grandma's a great cook—she makes the best lasagna and homemade breads. Sable's the only person who wouldn't want extra helping at Grandma's. That's because Sable hardly eats.

Sunday, 1-28

Friday, we had a fire drill during lunch. I guess you know that. It was freezing out, and no one had their coats with them. We found out later some kid trying to be funny pulled the fire alarm. I don't know if Mr. Gardner caught the person or not, but I bet half the school will be sick with colds tomorrow.

Those of us at lunch had to go out the doors near the gym parking lot. The teachers yelled at us to get over in the grassy area; today it was all covered in snow, but the teachers didn't care, all they wanted to do was stand together and talk. I got stuck walking out next to Nate and his friends. I tried to hang back before he saw me, but he did anyway. Once we got outside and away from the teachers, he walked over to where me and Allen were standing.

"Hey, just so you know, Man-boobs, Whitney's sick of seeing your butt cheeks every time you bend over in lab. It'd be nice if you wiped your ass every once in a while, too." All his buddies laughed but some of the girls nearby stared at the ground. I think they were embarrassed as much as I was. What Nate says hurts but sometimes it's what people don't say that lasts longer. I think they feel sorry for me. Or maybe they wish I'd fight back. But I can't. It would just get worse if I say something. Or I would get majorly pounded.

Anyway, I have lots of HW tonight so I can't write too much.

Oh yeah, I forget to mention that my sister's boyfriend, Danny Miller, the computer geek, came over today and he was coughing. I asked him if he had distemper, and he said, "Shut up, Chunko." I don't think he knows that dogs get distemper. For once, my sister heard him. She told Danny, "Be nice. That's my brother. I can get rid of you easier than him." Sometimes she can be okay. It wasn't the most wonderful compliment but at least she recognized that she has a brother.

Tuesday, 1-30

Sorry I wasn't at school yesterday but I've been sick. Really sick. I got some bug that's going around in church, and by Monday morning, I was living in the bathroom. You don't want to know any details so I will skip that. So, my weekend stunk. Ha ha.

I did manage to do a little homework but not much. I stayed in bed all day. I had a lot of other homework and jazz band practice, but I'm caught up in my journal anyway. When I got sick, Mom took care of me. My sister told me that I better not give her the flu because she was going skating on Tuesday with Danny. I did have enough strength to tell her that if he got sick, she could take him to the vet. "Maybe one day, you'll catch a sense of humor," she said.

"I think I used your toothbrush this morning by mistake."

"Mom, tell Jimmy to go to sleep. Or at least to shut up."

Mom yelled at Jessica for being mean to her sick brother. I won that round. Then I played Super Smash Brothers and I was beating the computer so easily that I got bored. So I started counting the soccer balls on my wallpaper and that made me dizzy. My saxophone teacher called and asked where I was, and I heard Mom apologizing to him. I forgot to tell Mom my lesson was changed from Saturday to Monday. She still had to pay him half his fee. Dad said it would come out of my allowance but maybe he'll forget. He does that with Jessica sometimes. But she's better at whining her way out than I am. Oh well, not a great weekend. I'm better now but I sure have a lot of makeup work to do.

Wednesday, 1-31

I was going to write in my journal this morning but when I got to school, the power was out. Usually I sit in the cafeteria and do any homework I didn't do the night before. Out one day and it's crazy how much I missed. I needed to do another journal entry and buy some breakfast. Well, I didn't get to do either. It was too noisy. And too dark. Everyone was told to go in the cafeteria, so it got really crowded in there. And there were no biscuits, which made it worse. Even though I'm watching my weight, if I don't eat anything before school, my stomach growls in class. I've dropped another eight pounds, which brings the total to twenty-four pounds. Allen and Paul say they can notice a difference, but no else has said anything. Actually, I have hardly any friends, so there's no one else *to* say anything.

While we were in the cafeteria, the teachers stood over by the windows. One of them did have a flashlight, but for a moment I felt that they were herding us up for something. Like a scene out of the old *X-Files* show, we were all about to be sold to aliens for food or forced to work in their mines. Every time a bus unloaded, the kids were funneled in with the rest of us. Every now and then, the intercom would come on with an announcement about the power. Someone asked, "How does that thing work if all the power is out?" It made me even more suspicious of the alien-food plot. And with me being bigger, I would be one of the first chosen.

When the power came back on, the teachers told us to go to class. And, there never was an explanation—there never is for anything in school. We go where we're told and do the HW we're assigned and sit when they tell us to sit. School is actually pretty easy if you aren't the kind of kid to question anything. So, when the lights came back on, everyone groaned.

Then, while we were walking to first period, the lights went out again. Everyone cheered. In about five seconds, they came back on. And we all groaned again. It was torture, like the principal was up front flipping switches so he could irritate us. If that was his plan, I can tell you it worked.

Anyway, my stomach wouldn't stop this morning in science. The class was quiet while we were doing a quiz on the periodic table and my stomach went "aaooooer." Or something like that. The kids next to me started laughing and then Mr. Mackey came over and asked them what was so funny. Then my stomach did it again. Mr. M looked at me and asked if I had a sick cat stuffed up my shirt. Well, that just got them to laughing more and pretty soon, I was too. Mr. M told us to do our quiz and walked away. All I could think about was eating—I don't know how I'll walk past the pizza at lunch today. I think my stomach hears the pizza calling my name.

<u>Friday, 2-2</u>

When I got to second period today there was a sign on the door saying we had to go to a different room. Mr. L's room had been broken into last night. I peeked through the window and the whole room was yellow. Someone had sprayed a fire extinguisher all over, and things were turned over. You probably know more about this than I do. But it was a big mess. We went to a room on the H-hall. When we walked in, Mr. L was sitting at the teacher's desk, slumped over and just slowly flipping the pages in his teacher's edition. He looked really hurt—his eyes were red and even after the bell rang, he wouldn't look up at us. After a few minutes, he called roll and told us to answer the Chapter Review questions. When he was sitting there, I could look at him without his noticing, and I saw him as a person not a teacher. That was the first time I ever pictured a teacher as a kid like me, having good days and bad days, sitting in class, worrying about grades, and even getting picked on.

Finally, Billy Dryden asked what happened to the room. It took Mr. L a minute to react, but then he told us that whoever it was broke out the window and crawled through. He said that they threw a chair into the TV and pushed everything off his desk. The fire extinguisher was sprayed over everything like I thought.

All of a sudden Whitney remembered the aquarium. "Oh, no, what about the goldfish?" she asked. Mr. L looked over at her and rubbed his forehead. I knew what he was going to say when he did that. "The fish are dead. I had to throw them out this morning. They sprayed down in the tank, knowing it would kill them." As bad as it was about his room, when he said the fish were dead, we all felt even worse. Every day, we would take turns feeding them. There were three, two orange and one mixed with white, and they would squirm at the top waiting to be fed. If I ever had a bad morning, sometimes I would watch the fish and my mind would go blank. I could forget about Nate and Whitney and all the rest and just pretend I was swimming around in there like Goldy and her two buddies.

One day, Mr. L caught me daydreaming and when he called on me, I had no clue what he'd asked me. So, instead of saying I wasn't listening, I said yes. Turns out he asked if I had ever been to New York and after I answered yes, he asked when. I said, "When what?" He said, "When did you go to New York?" and I said, "I never have, sir." Of course, everybody laughed and I didn't know why until later. I felt real stupid but probably deserved it this time. What I'm really saying is that I am going to miss the goldfish. I think Mr. L is too.

Monday, 2-5

We got our four-week grades and you'll be glad, I hope, to hear that I have 4 A's and 2 B's. I'm glad I'm in Health class and not PE this time. It's a pretty cheesy class, but at least I don't have to dress out. I'm really excited that I don't have to take PE anymore for the rest of the year. Maybe for the rest of my life! And I lost three more pounds! Yay! That's almost thirty pounds of fat gone.

I think I can bring up my history and science grades but it will take some extra work. Dad says he'll buy me a season pass to Kings Island if I get all A's. That would be too sweet. They have the best cotton candy in Cincinnati there. And the rides are the scariest. I remember one time when I had way too many corn dogs and then got on the Wheelie. It goes up and around like a Ferris wheel but it tilts up for most of the ride. Boy did I feel bad. I didn't throw up but I'm surprised I didn't. I thought that ride would never end. A kid from youth group was in the little car with me, and he was worried more than I was that I would get sick. He kept saying, "Don't you hurl on me, Winterpock. I'll have to go home if I smell like puke." His concern about my stomach pain was comforting. Not.

Anyway, this school is a little harder than my other one, but my teachers are good so that makes up for it. Even Mr. L in math is not as boring anymore. Maybe I'm just used to him now. It's still hard though for me to stay awake on Mondays when he has the overhead on and it's dark all period. Kids ask me for help at lunch now because they know I can do math pretty well. We have a couple of seniors in algebra—Robb Thuman and Adam Jones. Robb seems to be trying, but Adam doesn't work very hard. He misses lots of days and Mr. L tells him that he might not graduate if he doesn't get to work. I heard Adam say that if he could graduate, he'd join the Army and never come back to Cincy. He just wants to get as far from here as possible which probably means as far from home as he can. It's awful that someone feels that way about home. I try to help him when he asks me questions during class. He always wants to copy my homework, but I never let him. It won't help him on tests anyway. I see him in my lunch period when he's not skipping and going to White Castle. He keeps getting ISS when he gets caught, which is most of the time. You'd think he'd learn but I guess that goes with everything else in his life.

Tuesday, 2-6

Band class is the only good thing about school, except English. I've been playing the sax for about four years. Not non-stop though, ha ha. My sister hates it when I practice in my room. Mom thinks I'm really good at it. My band teacher suggested I go out for marching band next year. I'd really like to. The uniforms are cool, and our band has won several state awards.

My favorite music is jazz. I can listen to it for hours, especially if I'm bummed. It helps me forget my problems, at least for a little while. That's why I was so glad I made the jazz band. It takes up a lot of time, but I don't care. Jazz band is really cool, and even though I know a few of the kids laugh at me, we get along because we all love playing. I know the band respects me because I can really hit some great notes on the sax, but outside of band, some of the same kids act like they don't see me. I just don't get it—most of them are as geeky as I am. Only there's one difference—none of them are fat.

Guess that ruins my chances of ever getting in a rock band, which I would really like to do. I mean, can you imagine an overweight Eminem or Michael Jackson? But Jack Black's not exactly skinny, so maybe there's hope. With all the snow lately, I'm working out inside more.

Wednesday, 2-7

Please Don't Read This Page

Today in science Whitney was late to class and she had to sit in the seat behind me. I could hear her cursing under her breath after she sat down. I think she got a detention. A few minutes later she touched my shoulder and asked to look at my worksheet answers. She said she wanted to make sure hers were right since she knew I was making an A. I handed it to her, and then turned back around. I heard her scribbling, so I looked back and she was writing all my answers down. She had nothing! I told her not to copy my paper, but she wouldn't give it back. About then, Mr. M. called on me to answer a question. I told him I didn't have my worksheet, since I didn't want to rat out Whitney. He looked at me funny and said he was surprised. I hated lying to Mr. M, but I thought it might help Whitney be nice to me. When Mr. M turned around to write our new definition words on the board, I reached back to get my paper and Whitney had her cheeks all puffed out big. Nate was laughing at her and looking at me. Then she saw me and blew out air real loud. Even though I had let her borrow my paper and then lied for her, she still made fun of how big I am. I don't care if we get in trouble if you accidentally read this. Well, actually I do, but I thought someone needed to know how Whitney is. She's not the perfect little student all her teachers think she is, especially when Nate's around.

Sunday, 2-11

Please Don't Read This Page

This weekend I spent the night at Paul's. It was a total disaster. No, we didn't do any spying on the murder suspect. Paul hasn't mentioned that for weeks; he's been pretty bummed ever since his last girlfriend ditched him. All he does is talk about his girlfriend, and how she screwed him over. My parents were reluctant to let me go at first, but then gave in.

They want me to have a social life, even though they worry about Paul and his parents. It wasn't too bad at first—his parents have moved permanently upstairs with his uncle. They only come down in the basement to get stuff out of boxes and the refrigerator. I guess the fighting got so bad, Paul's uncle took pity on him, and let Mr. and Mrs. Grove sleep upstairs in one of the spare bedrooms. So his parents pretty much left Paul and me alone. We ate pizza and watched TV for a while, and then Paul wanted us to sneak out to a party. I got scared and didn't want to go. Paul said his parents and uncle were drinking and would eventually pass out for the night. Then we could sneak out. Paul kept running to the top of the basement stairs, opening the door and checking. When all the adults were finally out of it, he begged me to go with him. "It's just a few blocks away—it's not like we have to steal my uncle's car or anything." I told him my parents wouldn't want me to go, and I didn't want to break their trust in me. Paul said what they don't know won't hurt them, and then practically started crying. "Please, Jimmy, you're my best friend. We won't stay long. I promise."

I finally gave in. My heart was beating really hard as we slipped and slid on the icy street, but Paul was laughing. He took a joint out of his pocket. After a few hits, he asked me if I wanted some. I said, "No way. I don't think you should smoke that stuff either."

"It makes me feel sooo good," he said. "Like I don't live in my uncle's basement with screwed up parents who hate me."

We walked a few blocks and then cut through a couple of yards before we came to a street lined with cars on both sides. We could hear music blasting and loud voices. The party was at a kid's house who's in my sister's class, and for a split second, I was worried that she might be there. But I should have given my sister more credit. The parents must have been gone somewhere, because there were kids all over the house carrying six-packs and vodka bottles. Almost everyone there was smoking cigarettes or pot. A few kids were sniffing something through straws. I think they were doing cocaine. The bedroom doors were closed and Paul warned me not to open them because kids were having sex.

Paul introduced me to some of his friends, and they were cool. One kid made a comment about my weight, and some of the others laughed, but they weren't mean about it. Someone offered me a beer, but I didn't take it. I stood around and watched, trying not to let anyone see how shocked I was. I had heard kids at school talking about parties and getting high, but I didn't know it was this bad. Then I saw Whitney. She was drunk out of her mind. She saw me too. She came over and actually talked to me. She was nice at first, probably because she was drunk. Then one of our football players came over. "Hey, you trying to hit on her?" he asked me. He turned to Whitney. "This fat kid's trying to make out with you. You want me to rip his head off?"

"I was just talking to her," I said. "I wasn't doing anything."

"You're weird, man. Who invited you?"

"I invited him," Whitney lied. She licked her lips real slow and eyed me up and down.

"I want to see who has bigger breasts, me or you. C'mon, Jimmy, let's see." Then she yelled for everyone to come over and vote. A crowd gathered around us and Whitney pulled her tee shirt over her head. All the guys cheered because she didn't have a bra on. I couldn't stop staring at her. I mean, here she was drunk and exposed in front of a bunch of idiots who didn't know how smart she was. They didn't know she was saving for a telescope. All they saw was some hot girl they might score with that night. Especially since she was drunk out of her mind. I don't think Whitney would have done that sober. She finally pulled her shirt back down, and then the jocks started yelling, "Jimmy! Jimmy! Jimmy! Shirt off! Shirt off!"

When I refused to take it off, a group of jocks surrounded me and pulled it up. Everyone was laughing and yelling that I had the biggest tits. Even Paul. I didn't want anyone to see me crying, so I ran outside and walked back to Paul's house.

His parents were still passed out when I got there, so I went downstairs and lay on my bed and cried. Then I prayed. I prayed that my parents would still trust me. I prayed for forgiveness. And I prayed for Paul. I prayed for Paul's parents to get better. I prayed that Paul would be the same carefree kid he was when I first met him.

My prayers didn't work very well. I woke up to a bunch of yelling and screaming. When I checked my watch, it was quarter till three. It took me a minute for my eyes to adjust and then I saw Paul wasn't in his bed yet. Then I heard Paul's voice. "I hate you! You have no right to yell at me. Where do you think I get it from? My alcoholic parents, that's who." The screaming got louder, and I was scared. I didn't know what to do. Should I pretend to be asleep or go up and help Paul?

I finally decided to go upstairs. I don't know where his mom was but Paul's dad had his hands around Paul's shirt collar, banging his head into the wall. "Stop it!" I yelled. "You're going to hurt him."

Mr. Grove dropped Paul and stared at me. His eyes were red and angry. I thought he might grab me next, but instead he started laughing.

He turned to Paul. "Now you've got your fat friend taking up for you." It didn't hurt my feelings, because people pick on me all the time, though it seemed strange coming from an adult.

Paul was sitting against the wall bawling his eyes out, so I sat next to him. He kept saying he was sorry about what happened at the party and we shouldn't have gone. I was glad Paul was okay and that his dad didn't beat him up too much. But then I was scared. Scared of the rumors that would go around about me at school. Scared that my sister would find out and tell my parents. But then I forgot about me and I told Paul that things would be okay. But I knew better.

The next morning, my dad picked me up and took me to church. I was pretty quiet all day, and when we got home, he asked me if something bad had happened at Paul's. My conscience got the better of me, and I told him about going to the party. I didn't tell him about Whitney and what the kids said to me and why I left the party early, because I didn't want him to worry. I just told him the basics. He was really cool about it. He said he knows I only went to the party because of Paul, and he's glad I tried to help him. Now I'm not allowed to go to Paul's house anymore, but Paul can come over any time he wants. I'm lucky to have such a cool dad.

Monday, 2-12

Please Don't Read This Page

No one mentioned the party to me at school, though I heard a few kids snickering behind my back. That could be the normal everyday snickering though. And when I think about it, no one would say anything about me to my sister, because even an idiot would know that would make her mad. I can hardly look at Whitney in science class. After seeing her drunk, she doesn't seem pretty to me any more. Come to think of it, she was really nasty that night. She smelled like smoke, and her hair was stringy and messed up. I bet she's hurting inside just like Paul; otherwise, she wouldn't get so drunk. She reminds me of the way Sable was at youth camp last summer, not the drunk part but the hurting part.

I don't have excuses like other kids with addictions—my parents would do anything for me. That makes me more determined than ever to stick to my diet. Not that it's a real diet, I just have to watch my choices and portions. I'm amazed that it really works—that and the running and the Total Gym workouts. I actually lost five more pounds this week. The more I lose the more motivated I am. I can feel a difference in my body and the way my clothes fit. I've lost close to thirty-five pounds—only twenty-five more to go!

Not that it's been easy. I mean, I hate feeling hungry, and my body craves candy and Big Macs. I have to deal with it if I ever want to get all the fat off. I keep falling off my diet, and then I hate myself. Then that makes me want to go on an eating binge. It's a vicious cycle. Sometimes I wonder if it's worth it. Then I think of Paul and his parents. And I think of my own mom and dad, and I don't wonder any more.

Tuesday, 2-13

Here's a poem I wrote about pollution. I never thought poetry was very cool until this year. I used to think poetry was all about flowers and shepherds running through the fields and only girls like it. I didn't realize it could be about anything, and you don't have to use capital letters or punctuation if you don't want to. I like what you said about how in poetry one word can mean a whole paragraph. If you count the meaning behind the words in my poem, this should equal at least three pages.

Pollution
Looking over man's sin against nature,
A lone warrior stands at the edge of a cliff.
The sun obscured by stark, ugly monoliths,
He watches the world turn into a concrete killing field.
Between the cracks of decayed gravity,
He falls away from the planet.

Thursday, 2-15

Please Don't Read This Page

I used to like Valentine's Day, because of all the candy and cookies teachers gave out in elementary and middle school. Now it seems kinda cheesy. You can buy single carnations at school and then send them to someone. Some of the girls got a bunch. Even some of the guys got carnations. I don't have a girlfriend, so I didn't send any. I thought about sending one to Sable, but then she'd have to tell who sent it and it probably would embarrass her.

I've put back on six of the thirty-five pounds I lost. Ever

since the party, I've been really depressed. Spencer doesn't come around any more and has even started hanging out with Nate. Allen thinks Spencer's a real jerk and that I should say something to him. It won't change things—Spencer doesn't want to be seen with a fat geek with "man-boobs." It gets harder and harder to go to school. Kids laugh at me all the time and call me names to my face. They have to notice I've lost weight. Are they just getting in their last digs before I'm skinnier than them? Except for Allen, Sable and Paul, everyone treats me like I have leprosy. I asked Mr. M if Allen and I could eat lunch in his classroom, because it's too noisy in the lunchroom. He said it would be okay, as long as we brown bag it. That helps in some ways, but in other ways it makes us feel even more apart. Allen encourages me to stick to my diet, even though he eats junk food all the time. "You're more disciplined than me," he said. "So you have a chance at losing the weight. I'm doomed to be fat."

I saw Sable at youth group tonight. She asked why I didn't eat in the lunchroom any more. I shrugged and said that I hated it in there. She asked me to hang out with her and her friends in the lunch hallway. "We never eat the school lunches. They're gross. You're not supposed to eat in the hall, but kids do anyway." I told her I might do that, but I don't feel comfortable around her friends. They're what you call "emo," and they're considered really weird. I don't think they'd like me any more than anyone else. They might be even worse, since most of them are vegans and probably think I'm committing murder every time I eat a cheeseburger. Paul used to hang out with them the few days he showed up for school. He skips all the time now. I don't know how he gets away with it. The school usually calls when you're not there, but maybe his parents have given up on him and don't care whether he goes to school or not.

I tried faking sick this morning, but Mom took my temperature and said I was fine. She seemed worried about me though and asked if things were going okay at school. Dad asked the same thing, since I hardly speak any more when we run together. I don't know why I waste my time working out when I get picked on just as much, if not more. My life really bites right now.

Friday, 2-16

Please Don't Read This Page

Today was the worst day of my life. Much worse than last weekend. It probably happened because of the party. I mean, once kids get on a roll, it's like they don't know when to stop.

I wish I could run away from here forever. It's not just the same old jerks at school—I expect most of them to make fun of me, but when someone you thought was a good friend betrays you, then that's when it really feels bad. Like you begin to wonder what's wrong with you, if you really are a freak. You begin to think you deserve all the mean things that people do to you. You begin to feel that your life isn't worth much. That no one but your family will ever like you, and without them your life will be constant torture. I feel so bad. I can't understand why everyone hates me so much. I'm not perfect, but I'm basically a pretty good kid. I try to have faith in God, like our minister says. But right now I feel abandoned by Him. Why can't God be fair? Some people have it so easy—it's like the world was made just for them. They have it all, like Spencer.

I don't understand why Spencer set me up. He knows how tough life is for me. And he has everything in the world a guy could want. He's a star athlete, gets good grades, the girls like him…I mean, why would he go out of his way to hurt someone, when he has so much? I should have been suspicious; Allen warned me about him. He hasn't paid any attention to us since before Christmas. But, when he came up to me and said the soccer players think I'm cool and want me to keep stats for them this season, I was all over it.

"Come down to the locker room when you're done with lunch," he said.

You can guess how pumped I was. The soccer team wanted me to keep stats for them! Yay for me, I thought. Finally, I would have some respect around this school. I practically inhaled my lunch—I couldn't wait to get down to the locker room. But looking back, Spencer seemed nervous when he was talking to me. He had his hands in his jean pockets and he shifted his eyes away from me. I noticed he seemed different but thought he was stressed about a test or something.

When I got to the locker room, Spencer was nowhere around, just a few of the other soccer players. I didn't know them since they were sophomores, but I recognized them from the pep rallies. They asked me how things were and I said okay. One pretty big kid, probably a goalie, said I had to stay and watch what Sean was going to do. Sean was in his underwear, and he was about to run out into the hall and then back in the other locker room door ten steps away. One guy opened the door and watched while someone else was ready to push open the other door for him. Sean counted to three, sprinted down the hall, and then ducked back in the other side. Only a couple of screaming tenth grade girls saw him but no teachers. Everyone laughed and high-fived him. Then one of the players asked if I wanted to do it. I said, "No way" and grabbed my math book. That's when another player got in my way and said that if I'd try it, they would make sure that no one bothered me anymore. What a great thing to gain for five seconds of anxiety! So I took off my pants and everybody got by the door ready for me to go. One guy standing there said, "It's clear. Now!" Off I went right into a bunch of girls coming back from the gym. They screamed and so did I. I turned around to run back in, but the door was shut. And locked. I could hear kids laughing on the other side. I ran to the other door and someone was pulling on it, so I couldn't get in. I was stuck in the hall with no pants on. The weight room door was open, so I ran in there and hid in the corner. About ten minutes later, Coach Bronner came to get me. "C'mon Winterpock," he said. "There's no one out here." For once he felt sorry for me. I was late to HR but he gave me a pass. By the time I got on the bus to go home, the whole school had heard about me streaking in the hall. I hate high school.

Sunday, 2-18

Please Don't Read This Page

Paul and I hung out at McDonald's after church. I told him about the streaking episode and how the soccer players got a big laugh out of it. He told me he's thinking about running away from home and that I could go with him. Then people wouldn't be able to hurt us anymore. I told him, "Home is fine, but it's school I want to run away from."

He heard from some guys about jumping trains and traveling all over the country. He really wants to go out West or to Florida. Gee, my life's pretty bad right now, but not that bad. I don't really think Paul will run away; I think it makes him feel better knowing he has that option. His home life is really crazy. It's bad enough that his dad is a big jerk, but then his mother is out of it all the time. I don't get it. Guess she didn't get the mother gene or something. I mean, mothers are supposed to be nice and there for you—not that dads aren't that, but they aren't as soft as moms. They let you get away with more, because you'll always be their little kid. Mothers should be happy to see you and want to hear all about your day, not passed out drunk on the couch in the middle of the afternoon. Isn't there some sort of natural hormone that make moms want to treat their kids right? Last year we read the story *A Child Called It*, and it was about a mother who tortured her kid. That story seemed unreal to me at the time. I don't think Paul's mom is that bad, but still she's really two-faced. I mean, Paul's mother acted like an everyday, normal mom when I used to see her at church. But at home, she drinks herself into a sad state and then takes her anger out on him. Sometimes she gets so drunk, Paul has to hide her bottles. When she can't find any of her liquor, she has a big fit and throws things all over the place. Paul said she was so drunk one Christmas, his dad got upset and threatened to kill himself. When Paul told his dad everyone would miss him, his dad punched him in the face.

Even at his uncle's house, it's a struggle for Paul. There's always trash and dishes everywhere, and cigarette butts and gin bottles all over the living room. No wonder Paul wants to run away. Plus, his uncle brings different women in all the time and Paul can hear them "doing it" at night, because his uncle's bedroom is on the first floor, right over Paul's room in the basement. And his uncle's old, he's in his forties. It makes Paul want to puke. He thinks his only escape is drugs. I asked him if he was doing harder drugs, but all he said was "I barely get a buzz from toking up."

A lot of kids smoke pot—even some of the really smart ones—and they seem like they're fine. For most kids considered "potheads," it's pretty easy to tell they're smoking. In gym class I even heard some of the football players talk about getting high this weekend. If I wanted to, I could report them, but I would rather stay far away from those guys. I don't smoke because I hate what it does to your lungs, and I wouldn't want to hurt my parents. Besides, I would probably cough all day long. And from what I hear, lots of parents still smoke pot, so why should they be surprised when their kids do?

I tell Paul all the time that drugs won't solve his problems with his parents. That they'll only make things worse. But Paul just laughs and calls me clueless. "If you had parents like mine, Winterpock, you'd do drugs too. It's not like I can't stop or I'm addicted or anything. I just like the way they make me feel."

"How do they feel?" I asked.

"Sort of like happiness." Then he started laughing so hard, I thought he was crying. Maybe he was.

Monday, 2-19

Please Don't Read This Page

Things have calmed down at school, especially since Allen and I don't go in the lunchroom anymore. Most of the time, we eat lunch in Mr. M's class unless he's not there; then we eat with Sable in the hall. I just go to my classes and go home. Even the picking on the bus isn't so bad, or maybe I'm just used to it. I did pass Spencer in the hall, but he kept his head down and acted like he didn't see me. I guess if you sink as low as I've sunk, there's nowhere else to go, so kids leave you alone. Coach Bronner did call me into his office after the locker room disaster and asked me a few questions about the soccer players. I told him it was just a joke and I fell for it. Then he asked if I thought my life was in danger. That really freaked me out. Especially with all the talk of dead Kimberly Taylor. I think her boyfriend played soccer.

"I don't think so," I said. "The guys seem pretty nice, except for the picking."

"Well, I sure wouldn't want to have to kick anyone off the team—we have a chance to go to state."

"I don't think you'll have to do that, Coach."

"If you keep losing weight like you have been, things will be better. But you know how some of these guys are."

"My dad's helping with that," I said. "We work out everyday."

"Well, keep it up." He pushed his chair back and stood over me. "Good luck, Jimmy." He stuck his hand out and I shook it.

It felt pretty good that for once Coach saw me as Jimmy and not the fat kid in class.

Tuesday, 2-20

Please Don't Read This Page

I finally told my dad about the soccer players and what they did to me. He was upset at first, but then he told me to pray. He said to pray for Spencer, because he must feel pretty bad about what he did. Dad told me God would help me through the rest of the year and that I must focus on what's important, like family, my friends, and grades. "You need to be strong, Jimmy, and get on with your life. Focus on the things that matter and forget about the things that don't. You'll be fine, son."

I'm taking Dad's advice. I'm focusing on my schoolwork and youth group. And Paul and Allen. And the Total Gym. And maybe Sable.

Thursday, 2-22

The poem we read in class was okay, but it's too old-fashioned. The poet spoke of riding through the woods and coming to a fork in the road. He chose the road less traveled and has been happy ever since. I get the meaning—it's better to take risks and try new things. But the poem made me think how different things are today. There aren't many peaceful roads any more. Most of our lives are spent on expressways and highways, speeding from one to place to another. Even on back roads, people drive like demons. Then if you go too slow, you run the risk of road rage with some driver yelling the "f" word and giving you the finger. You never have to think any more about which road to choose, because we have GPS and MapQuest telling us which roads to take. And drivers need to take the most traveled roads, since we have to find gas stations.

My parents said they remembered the poem from high school and they really liked it. The poem was more relevant back then, when there weren't so many cars on the road. I bet in twenty years the poem won't even be read in schools, which is a shame because the message is good. If more people followed the poem's theme, there wouldn't be such an oil crisis, and the government would stop ruining places like Florida and Alaska. I wonder though, if everyone took his advice and went down the road less traveled, wouldn't it become the road most traveled?

Saturday, 2-24

Hi, Miss Pope. I wrote another poem—I'm not really sure what it means—it just came to me.

Pot, cocaine, speed
Drunk, Lost, Isolated
iPods, Computers, Cell phones
No one to talk to
Parents working
Teachers stressed
It's just a matter of time
Guns, knives, bombs
Before we self-destruct

On the news today, they played a video that some girl recorded with her cell phone at her school. It showed one girl attacking another girl in the hallway. Our school bans cell phones, but there are so many kids with them, it's impossible for teachers and administrators to do much about it. They'd have to bust 90% of the school. In the movies, robots rebel against humanity. But with the way kids treat one another, who needs Terminators? If you look at the halls, all you see are kids with iPods in their ears—no one talks to one another. Most parents—not mine—don't care if their kids play Wii twenty-four hours a day or sit around playing their iPods all the time. Teachers, like you, try to get their classes to discuss things, but everyone just sits there, as if you asked them to recite the quadratic formula. It's not a reflection on you, it's just that kids aren't used to discussing things. Their parents probably don't encourage them to talk like mine do. They make my sister and me sit around the dinner table, even if it's late, and talk about our day. I like it, but my sister sometimes rolls her eyes and acts bored. My parents don't notice it, but I do, and it makes me mad. She doesn't know how lucky she is to have Mom and Dad. My mom says someday Jessica will appreciate all of us, even me. Maybe when she's 110.

Monday, 2-26

Please Don't Read This Page

I'm worried about Paul; he's acting really manic lately. He's back in school and spends his time with the slacker kids. Paul's still smoking weed, not that his smoking makes me think less of him. I mean, lots of kids at our school have smoked it, but I'm worried he might have gotten into something more dangerous. Last week I saw him sitting on the ground between some cars in the parking lot. He was shaking but it wasn't because of the cold. I hope he hasn't jumped into any crazy drug that's going to kill him. He's one of the only friends I've got. There just isn't much I can do to help him, besides give him my time. I've never smoked or drank, so what do I know about what he's going through? He shouldn't be hanging with some of the people he's around. One of those kids, Ricky, went to jail for drinking and driving, and painkillers. He'd also gone to a gas station and stole gas. Paul's friendship with Ricky will only get him in trouble.

Wednesday, 2-28

My grandmother on my dad's side has really had a hard life. She lost her first husband, my grandfather, right after my dad was born. He died of lung cancer from working for years in the coal mines of West Virginia. After he died, my grandmother moved to Kentucky and lived with my great-grandparents. It was there that she met her second husband. He was really mean to my dad and believed in beating kids for little things, and my dad said he even hit my grandmother. So, she eventually left him and moved to Cincinnati, where she found a job working in a soap factory. She didn't make much money, but she provided for my dad. He did really well in school and got an academic scholarship to Ohio State. My grandmother always talks about how proud she is of my dad. She's had Alzheimer's for the past five years, and now she's gonna die but at least she always has a smile. She can't remember much, but she does remember loving my dad and me. Here's a poem I wrote about her:

Love
She remembers love
Loss
She remembers love
Stress
She remembers love
Divorce
She remembers love
Loneliness
She remembers love
Alzheimer's
She remembers love
Death
Love remembers her.

Saturday, 3-3

My sister asked me to go to the mall with her, since that's
the only way Mom would let her use the car. I said I would
go because I'm losing some weight, and my jeans are getting
kinda baggy around the waist. I'm not into wearing oversized
pants. It was still kind of depressing, because I really thought
I could find some cool jeans at Abercrombie, but they were
all too small, so back to Kohl's. My parents don't approve of
spending too much on jeans but said I could buy one expensive
pair if I really wanted them. They don't go for that status
thing—they think it's shallow and a waste. I agree, but I don't
think one pair of jeans will make me a follower. I just think
they're cool, and would make me feel like, for once, I fit in.
Get it? Fit in with the kids at school, because I can fit in a

status-jean that fat kids can't wear.

This weight thing is really getting to me. Seems like I take two steps backward for every one forward. I give up all the food I love, get up at five to work out and run with my dad, lose a little weight, then after a few days, I can't take the hunger pains any more, and chow down on a bag of chips. Or bribe my sister into sneaking me a Big Mac, or eat an entire bag of Oreos. It's amazing that I've lost any weight, especially with the zillions of fast food commercials on TV. And then my sister is constantly cooking pizzas and leaving the leftovers on the kitchen counter. I told her I'm on a diet but she doesn't care. I think she wants me to stay fat; that way she can feel superior. She is so into herself, it's sickening.

Monday, 3-5

I had to miss church on Sunday because of band rehearsal. I was in the school auditorium by eight and we practiced almost five hours, with only a few breaks. We played through all of the songs several times and did some last minute touch ups. Then we pretended we were actually performing in front of an audience and did our show.

An hour later, we set up the chairs and stood backstage as parents and other audience members took their seats. My lip was numb from playing my sax for so long, but after the place filled up, I was full of excitement and took my chair in the front row with the rest of the sax players. Our first song was "The Judge." We started off a little shaky, but after the first couple measures, we picked it up and played the song really cool. Our next several songs, "Milestones," "Harlem Nocturne," and "Low Rider," went smoothly, except I fumbled a little on one of the sixteenth notes in "Harlem Nocturne." Between songs, the kid in the chair next to me whispered, "Way to go, Winterpock," but I just ignored him and continued playing.

We concluded with "Won't You Come Home, Bill Bailey," which was the best we had ever played it. After our last note, the audience gave us a standing ovation. We filed off the stage and walked back to the band room with kids patting one another on the back, telling one another, "Good job." For once, no one seemed to notice my weight, and I felt part of the group. We stayed in the band room for a few minutes while Mr. Berry, our conductor, said how proud he was of us. Later I met up with my mom, dad, and sister, who all hugged me and told me how great the show was.

Then we went out for an early dinner at my favorite restaurant, Don Pablo's, to celebrate. I ordered the chimichangas as usual, followed by fried ice cream. Everything was great and we were all having a good time, until my dad got a call on his cell phone. He usually doesn't keep it on when we're out, but he did then. Something just made him.

"Hmmm, wonder what the Reverend wants," he said as he looked at caller ID. He clicked it on and said, "Hello, Reverend. Are we in trouble for missing church today?" Dad listened for a few seconds and then he looked real sad. "Oh, no," he said. "God help him. How's Paul?"

It seemed like an eternity before he hung up the phone. He gave me a serious look. "I have some bad news, Jimmy." But I already knew that by his face.

"Did something happen to Paul?" I asked.

Dad put his hand on my shoulder. "It's Mr. Grove." My dad choked on the words.

I didn't know what to say. I don't know when, if ever, I've seen my dad so torn up.

After taking a few deep breaths, he continued, "Mr. Grove killed himself. Paul found him in the basement after school. His dad hung himself."

My heart wouldn't stop racing, and I punched the table. "That's where Paul slept," I cried. "He hung himself in Paul's room." His father was an asshole even in the way he died. I punched the table again, and then my dad put his arms around me, and we walked to the car.

Tuesday, 3-5

Sorry I wasn't in the best mood today—it's not just your class; it's all my classes. Ever since I heard about Paul's dad, I haven't been able to concentrate. Nothing makes sense to me any more, and nothing in school seems relevant to my life. What does the Missouri Compromise have to do with my life now? Why do I care about the Lincoln/Douglas debates, when life all around me is falling apart? Sorry, but I don't care about the Globe Theater with its trap door, or the "light" women propositioning men in the pit. I've always heard that *Romeo and Juliet* was a good play, but I don't care about it now.

I tried to call Paul a few times, but all I get is the answering machine. His dad wouldn't ever let him have a cell phone, so there's no way I can reach him. I'm really bummed about Paul.

Wednesday, 3-7

I wasn't in school today because of the funeral. It was awful.
Paul's eyes were all red and his mother kept her arm around
him the whole time. I could tell he wished she would leave him
alone, so he could run away and hide somewhere. Most of our
congregation was there, even though Paul's parents stopped
coming to church when Mr. Grove lost his job. My parents,
sister and I sat right behind Paul and his mother. There were
some other relatives sitting with them too—I recognized Paul's
uncle and his grandmother, his dad's mom. They all looked sad,
but no one was crying, except Paul. Paul's mom kept fidgeting,
like she was bored and couldn't wait to leave and get a drink.
She looked older, like some people you see in an old folks' home.
The ones with the sad faces.

The minister tried to say a few words, but what can you
say about a mean guy like that? He talked about how there
is a time for every season, like birth and death, and it's God's
will, not ours, that determines our time. I think that was a
backhanded way of saying that we shouldn't take our own lives.
No one spoke on Mr. Grove's behalf, so the funeral was short.
My dad was one of the pallbearers, and I could tell Paul was
glad my dad helped his uncles carry the coffin out of the church.
Paul was probably thinking, See, our family is not that screwed
up. Mr. Winterpock wouldn't be friends with a group of freaks.

Mom drove me and my sister home after the funeral. The
family didn't stay around to talk to anyone, so I didn't get a
chance to say hey to Paul. I wanted to tell him to call me or
something. Since there wasn't a wake, I was hoping to see him
after the funeral. But the family only wanted relatives to be

at the burial. It was okay for my dad to go, but not me. On the way home, Mom asked if we wanted to get something to eat, but for once I wasn't hungry. Neither was my sister. She's been better lately, and I'm glad she came to the funeral with us.

For the rest of the day, my sister and I sat around and watched *Dr. Phil* and *Oprah*. I never watch those shows, but for some reason it helped. My sister asked what I thought was going to happen to Paul now. I said he'd probably be okay, maybe better off, in a way. But I don't really believe that. I think Paul's going to have a really hard time and probably get worse into drugs. Even though he acted like he hated his dad, I think he really loved him and wished that his dad would have liked him better. Paul used to talk all the time about how one day his father's going to take him to see the Cincinnati Reds, and they're going to have hot dogs and peanuts and everything. But the meaner his dad got, the more that dream faded. And after Mr. Grove lost his job, Paul stopped talking about that dream. I worry about Paul. I worry that his mom will make him sleep in the basement where his dad hung himself. I worry that Paul's mother will drink more. I worry that I won't have Paul as a friend any more.

In *A Separate Peace* Gene says, "Nothing endures, not a tree, not love, not even a death, by violence." The line didn't mean anything to me until tonight. Nothing ever stays the same. One day Paul's dad was alive and now he's dead. Paul will never be the same again, and our friendship hasn't been the same for months. Maybe the last part of this quote means that Mr. Grove's suicide will be forgotten over time. Then people will remember who Mr. Grove was before he turned mean. I think it will take Paul a long time to forgive his dad, but he'll never forget. I know how much Paul wanted his dad to love him. Not in a big way, but in small ways. He said his dad never paid any attention to him—Paul told me once his dad didn't even know what grade he was in. That would suck, really bad, to have a dad like that.

Friday, 3-9

Sorry, I've been kind of out of it lately. Paul called me last night and said his mom's really out of control and he can't take it anymore. He asked his grandmother if he could live with her, but she said her hands are tied, because his mom has legal custody of him. Besides, she's pretty old and doesn't have a place big enough for the both of them. His uncle can't stand Paul's mom, either, and has asked them to move out. Paul's afraid they'll have to live in a shelter. My dad said he could find them a place to live, if Paul's mom would be willing to get help for her drinking. My dad even called her, but she screamed at him and used obscenities. He even offered to let Paul live with us, but his mom won't listen to reason. Paul told me he's thinking about running away. My dad thinks he's only talking, but I believe him. I know how bad his mother is. Since I found out about the suicide, I haven't been able to eat much. I lost six pounds over the last few days. Weird. Mr. Grove dies and I lose weight. I think that's ironic, but I'm not sure how.

Sunday, 3-11

The worst has happened. There's been another murder—another girl from Hanover County. She was murdered in the same way as the other girl. There was no way the arrested kid could have done it, since he's been in jail for months. Now

everyone's all scared and really mad at the police for taking
the easy way out and arresting the boyfriend. They should
have known he didn't do it. Now there's another girl dead. It
also came out in the news that the police intimidated the kid
and he got scared and that's why he confessed the way he did.
He still admits he had sex with Kimberly, but it wasn't in the
woods—it was at his house. His parents were out of town and
he and Kimberly had a lot to drink. He doesn't remember much
about that night because of how drunk he was. The police now
think after Kimberly left the house that night, the killer picked
her up. I don't understand cops. Why would they want a cheesy
confession from some poor kid who only confessed because he
was scared out of his mind? You'd think they'd want to find the
real murderer.

I called Paul to tell him he was right about the kid being
innocent, but his mother said no one has seen Paul for three
days. She was pretty upset about it and started crying. I told
her I was sorry, but that only made her worse. Once she calmed
down, she told me she was moving and for me to call Paul's
grandmother if I found out anything.

The whole thing freaked me out, and I thought about Paul
and his spying, and wondered if the predator got him. Man,
that really scared me, so I told Dad the whole story, well, almost
the whole story. I left out the part about Jessica and MySpace.
Then the next thing you know, Dad's on the phone to the police
and they tell us to stay put, because they're coming right over.

When they got here, they asked me a lot of questions and
why Paul and me thought it was that particular guy, and I told
them how we found him on the Internet, and the head cop got
all serious and told me I was playing with fire. And that Paul

and me might have been his next victims. I got all scared when he told me that. He said we should let them do their job.

I asked them if they thought that guy really was the killer, and they said he was one of many suspects. That some of the agents didn't think the boy committed the crime, even though he admitted to it, and were still out there trying to find the murderer. He said we might have screwed up the whole investigation. They made me promise to stay away from the case and mind my own business. Dad assured him that I would not go putting my nose where it doesn't belong. Again.

Then they asked me if I knew Paul was planning to run away. I told them I didn't have a clue. They acted kinda funny, like they didn't believe me. Anyway, after a real heavy stare, they said they think Paul will call me or send me a letter. I'm supposed to let them know as soon as I hear something. I asked them if they contacted any of his new friends, since we don't hang out as much as we used to. They said the other kids don't know where he is either. I sometimes wonder if he's dead; maybe the killer got him, but I doubt it. I think he went to Florida to watch some of the major league spring training games. He loves baseball and I think, since his father's dead, he decided finally to see a game. Florida is a place Paul would like, because the weather's always warm and it's near the ocean. He's never been on a family vacation, and I bet he decided to take his own, now that there's no chance for him to have a real family. But I'm not saying anything. I don't want the police in my driveway again. We have too many nosy neighbors as it is.

Monday, 3-12

Life seems weird without Paul. Everything looks so different to me. My sister feels bad for me, but she still makes sicko jokes. She accused me of being gay, because of how hard I was taking Paul's absence. I couldn't believe she said that to me. I mean, I have nothing against gay people, and that's not what I was upset about. It's just that she acts like if a guy has a good friend he really cares about, then he must be gay or have a problem or something. And that's not fair, because my sister gets really hurt and cries and stuff if one of her girlfriends doesn't include her in something, or doesn't call her back for a few days. Some years ago she was a real head case because one of her friends moved to Iowa. She wouldn't come out of her room for days. I didn't think she was weird or gay or anything—I thought she just missed her friend. Why can't guys do the same thing? Paul and I were real close and we shared a lot, some good, some not so good things. I always thought I could help Paul and maybe even make up for how bad his parents were. But I was wrong. I couldn't do anything for Paul, and now he's gone. That really bites.

Last night I sat in my room and tried to imagine what Paul was thinking. He must feel really scared and alone. He's probably freaked out by his father's death and has nightmares about him, especially finding his body like he did. I bet he finally bought a cell phone and dialed his mom, then hung up fast because he was afraid the police might trace his call. He's smart that way. He might go to a public phone and try to call her, but that might make him look suspicious. He wouldn't do anything to get noticed.

One summer my family went to Sarasota and there were some homeless kids downtown, trying to get money from the old rich people. We went to this one restaurant on Palm Avenue and sat outside to eat our pizza. This kid came up to this old couple sitting next to us and asked to borrow some money for an airline ticket home. He made up this story about how he was mugged and the only thing the robbers left him were the clothes on his back. He was on his way home from college, and he had stopped in Sarasota to hook up with an old friend. It turned out his friend was out of town, so he stopped to gas up his car, when some Hispanic guys attacked him. They stole his car keys, credit cards and cash. His parents were on a cruise, so he couldn't call them for help. He was stuck in a strange city without any friends and no money. He said he was desperate, but he didn't look so desperate to me. His clothes were all nice and neat, and he seemed pretty confident and cool. And, besides, someone who had been mugged would have been at the police station, not walking around Palm Ave. Anyway, this old couple bought this kid's gig, and gave him a fifty-dollar bill! The kid acted like he was going to cry, but I could see the gleam in his eye. His story had worked and he ripped off these old people. I could see Paul doing this. He could do a number on people—he learned how to lie and deceive by practicing on his parents.

Please Don't Read This Page

Sable asked about Paul at youth group last night. I told her everything, and then I started crying. She put her arms around me and held me until I stopped. I've never been held by a girl before—except by my mom or grandmothers—but I didn't feel awkward like I thought I would. It felt good to have a friend care so much about me. Sable said she knows all about pain. When we were alone, she rolled up her sleeves and let me see all the scars on her arm. She said she used to cut herself to relieve the pain she felt inside. The pain from the cuts helped her forget her emotional pain. She said she doesn't cut herself as much since youth camp last summer, when the counselor made her turn in her razors. But she thinks about it all the time. She says it's like an addiction. I asked her what she does to stop herself. She said she reads lots of books, especially books about cutters. She said that helps, because she lives *vicariously* that way. That means to live through someone else. I guess you knew that, since you're an English teacher. But then again, you're not supposed to read this page, so it doesn't matter anyway.

I can't believe it's that easy for Sable though. I mean, there's no way reading would keep me from eating a pizza if it were there in front of me. Sable says it's all about control—mind over matter. The more you deny yourself something you crave, the more control you have in your life. I wonder if control can be an addiction. I wonder if everything in life could be an addiction if you took it far enough. My dad even said some people are so addicted to religion they neglect their families, just like alcoholics or drug addicts neglect their families. The world is so complicated, especially when good things can be just as harmful as bad things.

Monday, 3-19

I really like Shakespeare. He's really cool, and he's funny. That stuff at the beginning about weapons and stuff is pretty dirty, but most of the kids didn't get it, so you don't have to worry. Sable will make a good Juliet, if we ever get to her part. Are we going to read the whole play out loud in class? If so, we need to pick up the pace. No offense, but Tony is all wrong for Romeo. It takes him forever to read. He didn't pay attention when you said read to the punctuation mark; he stops at the end of every line. I know he volunteered, but you're too nice. Sable's going to make him look really bad when she reads with him.

I like the part of Benvolio, the peacemaker. That fits my personality well, though I wish he had more lines. You said that when we get into it more, we're going to act out some scenes. I'm not sure about using those fake swords you showed us—that could be pretty stupid, waving cardboard and tin-foil swords around. Everyone will probably start laughing and miss the point.

Thursday, 3-22

Please Read This—You're collecting my row's journals this week.

I'm practicing my lines like you asked, though I miss playing Benvolio. I think it's a good thing Tony said he didn't want to read anymore. He really doesn't think it's a dumb play—he just said that to get out of reading. Tony knew everyone was complaining about him. Sable told me before class she was going to suggest that I read Romeo's part, but I was surprised when the rest of the class agreed with her. I heard someone whispering about my being too fat for the part, but someone else said, "Yeah, but at least we'll get through the play sometime this school year." Then one of the girls said, "He's not as fat as he used to be." But I think I was the only one who heard her. I'm down almost forty-four pounds, and now Mom's complaining about having to buy me new clothes. I can tell she's really happy about it though. Mom can't stand for me to be the only one buying new clothes, so she's losing weight too. My sister says she looks real hip, but she doesn't look any different to me.

I read ahead to the part you want Sable and me to act out, and I think they're supposed to kiss. There's something about Romeo and Juliet putting their hands together, and Romeo says, "O, then, dear saint, let lips do what hands do." Not long after that the stage directions say, "[*Kissing her*]." If I kiss Sable, the class will laugh and get way out of control. Do you think we could act out another scene? Also, I don't want Sable getting all mad at me. What if I accidentally kiss her too strong, and she thinks I'm taking advantage of the situation? I hope you're reading this. I wish I had looked ahead before I agreed to be Romeo. Now I'm stuck.

Monday, 3-26

The prayer scene went okay, and I only heard a few snickers from the back when I pretended to kiss Sable.

Have you noticed that I'm losing weight? Sable says I look really good. That makes running with Dad in the morning much easier. I feel embarrassed telling you this, but I think someday I would like to kiss Sable for real. Don't worry, I'm not going to kiss her in class or do anything stupid, it's just that I think I like her, I mean really like her, not just as a friend, but as a boyfriend/girlfriend kind of like. I would talk to my sister about Sable, but she would think it was a big joke and tell my parents, and then they would ask me a million questions about it, and I would feel all stupid and stuff. Maybe I'll see Sable at youth group on Sunday.

Wednesday, 3-28

Guess what, Sable just called and invited me over to her house on Friday night. She said we can just hang out and eat pizza—maybe we'll practice our lines for *Romeo and Juliet*. Haha. My sister heard me telling Mom about the phone call, and now she's teasing me about having a girlfriend. She keeps asking me stupid questions, like what am I going to wear, am I going to bring her flowers, am I going to kiss her. I really shut her up when I told her I already kissed her. Later, my mom asked me about Sable, and I explained about the scene in *Romeo and Juliet*. My mom laughed and my sister wanted to know what was so funny, but we just ignored her, which made my sister have a mini-tantrum. Then Mom and I laughed even harder, and my sister got in trouble for saying Sable and I probably had sex. There's no way that would ever happen, I mean we're just friends.

I wonder what kind of pizza she's gonna have. I don't eat pepperoni or sausage pizza anymore, just onion and green peppers. I wonder if I should say something about that, but I guess I don't have to since Sable's a vegetarian. And, then soft drinks. I don't even drink those anymore, not even diet ones. Guess I sound a little crazy about my diet, but I'm determined to lose sixty pounds by the end of the school year. I've lost a total of forty-six pounds, only fourteen more to go.

Thursday, 3-29

My mom said I could get contacts, especially after what happened today. Most teachers don't realize that the guys' bathroom can be a battleground. Or a torture chamber. Not only because kids can pick on you, but because of all the smokers. At middle school they had teachers standing outside the bathrooms, and if they smelled smoke, they'd go in like a SWAT team. Here, the teachers stay as far away from the bathrooms as possible. I can't say that I blame them, but with a school this big, the bathrooms can get pretty tough. Fights break out in there all the time, and kids can easily smoke and drink just about anything they want without getting caught. That's why I never go in there during lunch periods. But yesterday I couldn't wait, so I went in hoping no one would notice me. But guess who was in there? Nate and his henchmen. His English class just finished reading *Lord of the Flies,* so, you guessed it, Nate started in on me. "Hey, it's Piggy," he said.

"He looks more like a scrawny turkey than a pig," someone said.

But Nate continued. "What are you doing back? I thought you fell off a cliff and they stuck your head on a stick."

"Didn't you read the book?" I said. "It's your head that gets stuck on the stick, not Piggy's."

A couple of his friends laughed. I should have known

better than to try and make Nate look stupid, because he shoved me into the wall so hard, my glasses fell off. Another kid "accidentally" stepped on them. "Oh look, Piggy broke his glasses," he said. Then they ran out of the bathroom.

It makes me more determined than ever to lose weight. Fourteen pounds, fourteen measly little pounds, and I will have reached my goal. Who'll care about Nate and his thugs then? Not me.

Dad and I are now running three miles every morning, and I'm up to level three on the Total Gym. My goal is to get to level six like my dad. I'm getting stronger all the time, so my dad thinks I'll be up with him by summer.

Saturday, 3-31

Please Don't Read This Page

Sable's little brother is really cool. He's autistic and it doesn't seem like he understands things, but I think he does. Sable and I hung around in her basement and played board hockey, and her brother kept trying to get Sable to leave and come upstairs with him. I think he was jealous that she had a friend over. But then I let him play Sable, and he was awesome. He kept winning, so she gave up, and then he and I played. Every time he scored a point, he jumped around the room, punching the air and barking. When we finished, Sable put in *The Empire Strikes Back* and Jason—that's her brother's name—would say the lines before the characters did. Sable said he's memorized all the lines in every *Star Wars* movie. The kid is incredible.

Sometimes he really bugs Sable. I mean, she loves him

and all, but her parents give all their extra attention to him and expect her to do the same. That would really get to me, especially if it happened all the time. Sable finally yelled for her mother to get him. Her mother came downstairs with a veggie pizza, and Jason started yelling, "Give me pizza! Give me pizza!"

Instead of taking him upstairs, his mother tore off a piece of our pizza and gave it to him. Sable was really steamed. "Why do you always give in to him?" she yelled. "He'll never learn manners if you give him everything he wants."

Her mother looked really sad. "He doesn't understand things like the rest of us," she said. She practically had to drag Jason up the stairs because he didn't want to leave. While Sable's mom pulled him up the stairs, he threw the pizza on the beige carpet and then laughed about it. Sable was stuck cleaning up the mess. "He's much smarter than my mom gives him credit for. He knows he can get away with murder around her, especially if he acts all stupid. But he knows what he's doing. He acts different around me, but he's got Mom trained."

"Have you told your mom?" I asked.

"Yes, but she doesn't listen to anybody. She feels guilty about Jason, and thinks she caused all his problems. She smoked when she was pregnant and thinks that's why he turned out that way. When I told her she smoked when she was pregnant with me, and I turned out okay, she said that I should be grateful that I got lucky. Her whole world is Jason. It's really hard on Dad, because she's wrapped up in Jason. There's never time for me or Dad."

"Yeah, that would be tough," I said.

"My mother's wrong, anyway," Sable whispered. "I didn't turn out okay."

"You seem okay to me," I had to tell her.

"I hide lots of things. Things I'd probably tell my parents if Jason wasn't there. But I don't want to cause any more grief in their lives than they already have. Their marriage is shaky enough, as it is."

"But you're their kid. And they're your parents. Who else is going to help you when you need it?"

"I've been taking care of myself for a long time. I don't need anybody."

We ate our pizza and watched the movie for a while, then Sable and I went upstairs to get on her computer.

"You want to see some really cool stuff?" she asked when she connected to the Internet. Then she opened up a chat room for cutters. "There're some really cool kids here," she said. "You think I have issues, you should hear some of their stories."

"You said you were going to quit. I thought you stopped."

"I did for a few months, but then the urge came back. It's like I can't stop it. I try reading to get my mind off of it, and that helps some, but then the urge takes over my whole body." She looked away for a second. "I have to do it."

"No, you don't," I said, putting my hand on her shoulder.

I told her I didn't understand why anyone would want to hurt themselves that way, and Sable said she does it to get rid of the pain inside. When I asked her what the pain was, she said she couldn't tell me, maybe someday, but not right then. I asked her if it had anything to do with her little brother. She said in a way, but not really. She said I was really sweet and she likes hanging around me because I live in a safe world, the world she used to live in.

When I asked her what she meant by that, she said she

didn't want to talk about it anymore. But I did tell her she should talk to one of the counselors at school, like Mrs. Duffy (she's pretty cool—she's talked to me about Paul and everything) or one of our youth ministers. I told her that I had to fight my urges to eat all the time, but my parents have been a big help teaching me how to discipline myself. Cutting is not that much different from overeating—they're both bad for you. She can hide her problems, but I can't.

Sable said she has control over her eating, but cutting is different. She said she hardly eats at all, because, for girls, even just a little bit of extra weight is bad. Talking to other cutters online has at least taught her why she cuts herself. Most cutters have been hurt on the inside, so the only way they can feel better is by hurting themselves on the outside, though Sable says it doesn't really hurt that much. It would hurt me, if I cut my arms up with a razor blade. I can't even imagine doing that. It makes me feel bad that Sable has so much pain inside. I told her that, and she said I was a really big help. I asked, "What do you mean 'really big'?" Sable laughed. But then she said she'd talk to Mrs. Duffy.

I felt so bad for Sable, I almost kissed her. But then she showed me her arms and it made me cringe, so I didn't think she'd want a kiss from someone as safe as me.

Monday, 4-2

I went to the eye doctor after school today, and he gave me some trial contacts. They don't feel as funny as I thought they would, though I need practice taking them out. After a bit, they started bugging me and I tried everything I could think of to get them out my eyes. I blinked and wiggled my eyes around; then the contacts got stuck on the side. I even banged the back of my head with my hands. Finally, I stuck my fingers in my eyes and pulled them out.

I hardly recognize myself. I mean, I really couldn't see what I looked like without my glasses, because I'm practically blind without them. But my face doesn't seem as fat as it used to be. I'm beginning to grow cheekbones and a chin!

I feel more like Romeo now that I'm wearing my new contacts. And because of the weight loss. I mean, how realistic would it be for a fat, medieval kid to be an expert swordsman? Talk about an easy target.

The scene with Tybalt was really cool—I'm glad we watched that part of the video before we acted out that scene when Tybalt dies; otherwise, I think the class would have laughed at us. But after seeing the scene, everyone really got the feel for what the lines mean, and how upset Romeo was over killing Juliet's cousin. Like, how can she forgive him for that? Especially if Romeo doesn't get to her before her father does and explain that it was an accident. I don't get some parents. How can they keep kids apart who really love each other? Especially good kids. But I guess if they didn't, there wouldn't be near as many tragic love stories.

Tuesday, 4-3

Please Don't Read This Page

Sable had a really bad night last night. She called me crying hysterically, saying that she cut herself again, but this time there was blood all over the place and she was afraid she went too deep. "You better get your parents," I told her, "so they can get you to the hospital or call 911." She kept screaming, "No! No! You don't understand! I want to die!" I was really afraid for her, and kept her on the phone while I went downstairs to get Mom and Dad. It was after ten and they were half asleep on the couch. I went to wake them up, but then I heard Sable's mom in the background. It was awful, because I could hear how shocked her mom was when she saw all the blood and her cut arms and everything. Right before Sable hung up, I heard her dad yell, "My God! My God!"

Sable wasn't in school today and I'm not sure if I should call over there. But I want to, because I don't know if she is alive or not. Mom offered to call her house for me, but I think I should be the one to call. Life seems so strange to me now. I mean, I have two close friends and I don't know whether either one of them is alive or dead. I can see having one close friend that you might not know about, but two?

At least I know Allen's okay. When I saw him in the lunchroom today, I really ripped on him about his grandpa's shoes. It was like I needed to feel like a normal guy again. Allen joked about how my head was shrinking because I'm losing so much weight. He asked if he could have all my hats since they don't fit me anymore. It felt really good, kidding around with Allen.

Wednesday, 4-4

Please Don't Read This Page

It sucks that Sable won't be back for two weeks. It's not as much fun reading the parts with Katie Poole, even though she's a good reader. To me, Sable is Juliet. I don't mean I like Sable the way Romeo likes Juliet. He really overdoes it with all the metaphors and similes and stuff. It's just that Sable and Juliet have the same soul. They're both really deep and notice things like the stars and the moon, and both believe in fate. Juliet can't communicate with her parents; neither can Sable. And, like Juliet, Sable acts on her feelings without thinking about the consequences. And, they both cut themselves. Weird how things that happened hundreds of years ago are still happening today. Like girls hurting their bodies, kids picking on each other, parents abusing their kids, people fighting over stupid things...and then dying over it all.

Thursday, 4-5

Everyone's noticing how much weight I've lost, but some of the kids still treat me the same. Like Nate. He keeps laughing and calling me a loser. "Now he's REALLY a big loser," he said in math. Mr. L just ignores him and lets him get away with it. I think Mr. L is afraid of Nate. I guess I can't say I blame him. Nate is one of those kids who could get the whole class against a teacher and make the teacher's life miserable. Nate only goes so far, then pulls back, so if the teacher ever called his parents, Nate could easily say Mr. L has it out for him. Then his parents would try to get Mr. L fired. Kids can be really manipulative that way. I don't know why anyone would ever want to be a teacher. They have to take so much off of kids and hardly make any money for it.

Most of the students drive better cars than the teachers. I mean, I know teachers, at least most of them, are dedicated and want to help kids and everything, but I still feel sorry for them, because most kids don't really appreciate what teachers are trying to do. They just want to get good grades, even if they have to cheat, so their parents don't give them a hard time. I mean, my parents really like that I get good grades, but they don't pressure me like I've seen some parents do. Maybe because they know I'm one of those kids teachers call self-motivated.

And things come easy to me. Like math. I think that's why I was chosen to tutor Robb Thuman. Me, of all people. He was starting quarterback on the football team this year and has been offered a football scholarship to Bowling Green. He needs to pass Algebra I and Algebra II to graduate—he never made up his Algebra I class and he's barely passing Algebra II. Since Robb's in my math class, Mr. L asked me to tutor Robb because I'm so far ahead of everybody. At first, Robb was a real jerk— almost as bad as he was earlier in the year—but when he saw I really could help him, he kinda eased up and started joking around about how clueless he is in math. "Man, I never could get this stuff. Teachers go way too fast for me. On the field, it's easy—in here, it's like I've got mush for brains." I keep telling him he can get it if he practices, just like he practices football.

"I can't practice by myself; I need a coach." I offered to help him after school, but I would need a ride home. Then he suggested that he come by my house later, after he drops his girlfriend off. "I have to pass this class, man, or I'll lose my scholarship. I'll do whatever it takes. Carly and I usually hang out after school, but I'll drop her off and then come by for an hour, if that's okay."

"Sometimes, I have to stay after for band practice, but otherwise that'll work."

"Maybe we can workout some. I'll help you get in shape, and you help me get smarter. I can't believe you're the same kid who ran around with his boobs hanging out earlier this year."

Man, things really have changed. The star football player of Hanover High is asking ME if I want to workout with him.

Saturday, 4-7

Can't believe it's time for spring break already. We're not going anywhere this year—my parents are trying to save more money for my sister's and my college education. My dad says we only can take two vacations a year—one at Thanksgiving and one in the summer. I don't mind, cause that means I'll have plenty of time for working out and my music. My sister's all moody though, because some of the juniors are allowed to go to Destin by themselves and rent hotel rooms on the beach. But my mother said, "No way!" Robb's going though—that's all he's been talking about for weeks. I told him not to forget everything we worked on. He's been passing more of his tests and he's really pumped about it. But he messed up big time over the weekend. Going home drunk from a party, he got a DUI. His dad had a cow and took his car away from him. So now my dad has to drop me off at his house for me to tutor him. My dad doesn't mind because Robb doesn't live that far away— I could walk, but my mom worries when I'm out alone at night because the murderer is still out there. She really needs to get over that. Like I'm going to get kidnapped or something.

I can't believe Robb's parents are still letting him go to Destin, especially after everything Robb's told me about what they do on spring break. "All we do is party. From the time we get up in the afternoon until we pass out the next morning. It's so awesome. Last year I went bungee jumping while I was high. That was so cool. And you wouldn't believe the chicks. They put out like you wouldn't believe. Then it's really party time."

"Your parents are letting you go after the DUI?" I asked him. "Why?"

"They know how it is; they partied all the time when they were in high school. And, it's my senior year. After I graduate, it'll be all football practice. Got to sow my oats while I can, Jimmy-boy." He Dutch-rubbed my head. "You have a lot to look forward to, man. You keep losing all that weight, you'll have the chicks after you too."

I can't see my parents letting me go anywhere that's not chaperoned, especially a place that's a thousand miles away and full of drunken kids. Maybe that's where Paul is—on the beach having a perpetual (Sable taught me that word) spring break.

Monday, 4-9

Sable called and said she's coming back to school right after the break. She sounded happy and rested, but I could tell she was embarrassed about what happened. "The doctors said I could have died. I didn't realize how deeply I cut myself—that's never happened before. Guess I'm lucky, huh?"

Sable said she's been in counseling every day and is

learning that her cutting has nothing to do with her parents or her brother. It's because of something that had happened to her as a little girl that she never told her parents about. She's still not sure she wants to tell them, but at least the doctor is helping her sort things out. All her parents do is cry and feel guilty. They can't believe how long she's been a cutter and they didn't even notice. Sable said she heard some of the nurses whispering about her mother and she let them have it. She used the word "confronted."

"How would you like to have a kid who has to read signs just to go to the bathroom? Not just once, but every time he goes. It's not easy. My mother does the best she can. She's too busy working and taking care of a husband and two kids to stick her nose in other people's business. You're nothing more than a conceited bunch of scandalmongers." I have to give it to Sable. She knows a bunch of really cool words.

I asked her if she was cured of her cutting disease. She said she has a long way to go, but at least she has a chance.

Thursday, 4-12

Guess what? Robb came back from Destin early. He and his roommates trashed their hotel room and were fined for damages. They came home because they ran out of money. Robb asked if I wanted to come over and hang out, watch a movie, anything but math. After my dad dropped me off, Robb said I should just spend the night so my dad doesn't have to drive again.

"Can't this time," I said. "I have church in the morning."

"Can't you skip it this once?"

"Not really. The minister said he needed to talk to me about something very important. He said to make sure I show up. Man, you look like hell," I told Robb.

"That's the first time I've ever heard you curse, dude. What's with you?"

"Nothing. That's the best way to describe how you look."

Robb tried to laugh it off, but I could tell he wasn't real happy about the wall-to-wall zits on his face. "Must have been all the vodka I drank. I think I'm allergic or something. My parents are making me go to the skin doctor tomorrow. Hey, you want to put a pizza in or something?"

Robb seemed glad to hang out with me; he ignored all his phone calls, even the ones from Carly. "Destin was fun and all, but it sure is good to get home—we had eight guys in a room and only three towels. It got nasty after a few days. I think I drank enough to last me for three spring breaks."

"Did something happen with you and Carly?"

"Don't mention that bitch's name to me." Then Robb went on about how Carly got drunk every night and flirted with every guy who looked at her. And how she got in a wet t-shirt contest and you could see everything. Then he caught her in bed with some redneck who was way older than she is.

"That did it, man. I'm through with that little tramp. Man, that really killed me." Then he put his fists on his head, and I thought he was going to cry. "I loved her, Jimmy. At least I thought I did. And she goes and does this to me."

Robb didn't bring her name up again. We played XBOX for a couple of hours, ate pizza, then my dad came and got me.

Sunday, 4-15

Today at church, my youth minister asked me to give a talk about all the weight I lost and how my faith helped me. He said he wanted me to speak spontaneously, from the heart and all. So, before I had time to think about it, there I was standing in front of Sable and the rest of the kids in my group with the minister smiling, saying, "Jimmy's going to speak today. His is a story of how faith in God can turn your life around."

All the kids started clapping and cheering, which gave me a minute to think about what I was going to say. The minister said to speak from the heart, and so I did. Sable recorded my talk and I transcribed some of it here. Hope this counts as a journal entry. Anyway, here goes:

"Hey, guys, thanks for the applause." (I take a deep breath here.) "I'm not sure my faith in God helped me with my weight loss, but my faith in God gave me faith in myself. Even when I was really big, and kids and adults laughed at me or didn't want anything to do with me, God always made me feel that I was a good person. That what I was on the outside didn't take away from who I was on the inside—a normal kid who just wanted to fit in. A kid who liked school, despite his tormentors, a kid with a family that really cared about him, a kid who wished he could play sports and loved video games. You guys really helped me a lot too. Some of you have known me ever since I was a little kid, and no matter how big I got you guys always accepted me. Maybe that's because you knew me as Jimmy, not as a fat freak. Our pastor spoke often at church about 'Judge not, lest ye be judged,' and I guess you all took that to heart.

"I don't understand people who judge others—God made

us all different so we wouldn't get bored here on earth. Since there are no two people exactly alike, you could spend your whole life judging. Isn't that what judging is all about anyway? Putting down people because they are different from you? But everybody's different, so it makes no sense to me. Of course, I was different from other kids in a BIG way." (Laughter)

"So I guess it was easier to judge me than most kids. It was when that judging turned into out and out meanness that I almost lost hope and faith in God. I even considered killing myself, but not for more than a few hours. God got in the middle of all that and saved me. He didn't speak to me directly, but he spoke to me through one of my best friends. God showed me that my problems were very small compared to other people's problems, like my friend Paul, who you all know. He faced bigger problems than me, problems harder to solve than losing weight. Another one of my friends couldn't keep from hurting herself, and in helping her, I learned to help myself. I realized that overeating was just as bad, not in the same way, but with the same consequences. It was then that I had another revelation—that I needed to educate myself about eating and exercise. So with the help of God, my parents, my friends and the Total Gym, I began to take care of my body. The kids picking on me didn't matter any more; what mattered was the realization that I was killing myself, only in a slow way. Suddenly, I didn't want to do that anymore. I had too much to live for. I wanted to feel good, try out for sports, learn about the world, but most of all, to be in good enough shape to do the things kids are supposed to do. Before I lost weight, I couldn't run, couldn't dive in a pool, couldn't climb the Great Bear Dunes with my family, and I would never be able to fly across the rain forest on a zip line, something I've always wanted to do.

"So, you can see, I've almost achieved my goal—And to be honest, I'm not sure how I got to be so big in the first place. All I remember is playing video games, learning my saxophone and then I look around and I'm a big, fat somebody else. It was like I was in a nightmare, not in control. My fat was a great big security blanket which kept me from participating in the world. But I thank God my family supports me; my parents are great people and would do anything for me. But sometimes things happen to us because they just happen. It's up to us not to blame anyone or give up. It's up to us to ask God for help to change our lives and get back on the right track. And that's what I learned from being a big, fat kid." (Applause) ("Way to go, Jimmy!")

Wednesday, 4-18

I've almost reached my goal, sixty pounds less of Jimmy. If I stand on the scale just right, I weigh 148 pounds—that's a loss of forty-seven pounds. Only thirteen pounds to go. I can't believe I managed to lose all that weight. All my teachers have commented on how good I look, even you. Thanks for the compliment, Mrs. Pope. The funniest thing that happened was when I went down to the gym to work out one day after school. (I had a couple hours to kill before a jazz concert). Coach Bronner walked by and when I said "hey," he stopped, trying to figure out who I was. "Do I know you, son?" he asked.

"I'm Jimmy Winterpock," I said. "Remember me, from PE? I'm the fat kid that everyone made fun of. Only I'm not so fat any more."

"No kidding," he said. "I never would have believed it if I hadn't seen it for myself. You look great, Jimmy. You don't look like the same kid."

"Well, I did get contacts," I said.

Coach laughed. "You got more than that." He patted me on the back. "Way to go, Jimmy. You won the game." He stared at me for a minute. "You need a spotter?"

"That'd be cool," I said.

Things have been happening to me like this a lot lately. I'm still the same kid on the inside, but my outside is different. Sometimes I look in the mirror and don't recognize the kid standing in front of me. The biggest change is in my face and chest. I've lost my "man boobs" and you can actually see the bones in my face. My balloon face has deflated into one with actual features. I catch my mom staring at me in the mornings when I'm at the breakfast table. My sister doesn't try to hide her astonishment. She puts her hands on my face and punches my back and keeps saying, "Oh, my god. Oh, my god. You did it. You really did it." But I understand. I can hardly believe it myself when I look into the mirror.

Thursday, 4-19

I can't believe spring break's over and we've been back in school for three days already. Robb's really scared, because he thinks he's forgotten everything he learned. We know he can do the problems when I'm there with him, but he says he's going to panic during the exam. "I just don't do well on tests. I don't care how well I know it, my mind blanks out. It gets all quiet and the teacher watches me like a hawk and it just freaks me out."

I told Robb he needs to pretend he's sitting at his kitchen table and forget about everything else. He had the brilliant idea of pretending he was in a classroom while doing problems at his kitchen table. He made his mom and dad leave the kitchen while I sat there staring at him like I was Mr. L, with puckered lips, bugged eyes and all. That didn't work very well because we both kept cracking up. Now Robb says he's going to crack up when Mr. L gives him the evil eye during tests. I told him I think that's better than sitting there all nervous. He said I just might have a point.

Saturday, 4-21

Yesterday, I went to the school baseball game with my dad. It was a great afternoon for a game since it wasn't as hot as last week. People know I've lost a lot of weight and I can see them looking. I can even sense that my dad is proud of me, but he never says much in public about it. We sat behind the screen on the third base side, where our team's dugout is. One neat thing is that the guy who threw out the first pitch was one of the Lost Boys of Sudan. I don't think he has ever played ball before, but he got it pretty close to the catcher. Everyone cheered for him when they announced him. My dad told me his story during the first inning. I can't imagine walking 1200 miles barefoot while being chased by lions and hyenas. The kid was tall and thin and his skin was the color of coal. His baseball hat was way too big and it hung down on his ears but he smiled a big smile anyway. When he walked by, I shook his hand. He seemed very gentle and from what Dad had told me about the Lost Boys, I think my struggle was nothing compared to his.

The game was a good one and we hit a home run in the bottom of the sixth to win. Roston High got the bases loaded in the top of the seventh, but we turned a double play to end the game. I think that if we can win the next few games, we get in the playoffs. I overheard some fathers talking about our players and one of them, Matt O'Connell, is going to Ohio State on a scholarship, which is pretty cool. Maybe he'll play for the Reds one day, and I can say I went to high school with him.

I didn't realize until halfway through the game that Nate and his dad were sitting in the next set of bleachers over. I saw Nate's dad look over at us while he was talking to Nate. The next inning, while the pitcher was warming up, his dad got up and started walking toward us. I got nervous and my dad sat up. When he got to us, he shook my dad's hand and then mine. He told me, "You should be proud of what you've accomplished this year." Then he turned to my dad and said, "And so should you." He kind of hesitated and looked real hard at my dad. "We all have our goals." When Nate's dad went back to his seat, my dad put his hand on my shoulder and then the game started back up. It feels good now but I hope I never forget the way it was. Otherwise, I might be right back there. All it takes is Little Debbies, Whoppers and ice cream.

No way.

Sunday, 4-22

We had a great time at King's Island yesterday. It was really cool, especially since it was just for freshmen. The rest of the school goes next week some time. I heard our class goes by itself because the freshmen class is always the largest. I don't know where all the freshmen go when they get older, maybe to special trade schools or they drop out, but ever since the school opened there have always been more freshmen.

Sable hung out with me and Allen, and we had lots of fun, even though waiting in lines all day was a pain. And it was hot. Allen couldn't go on any of the really fast rides because his heart doctor told him not to, but he stood in line with us until we got on. The roller coaster lines took forever to get through; I think we talked about everything we know by the time we got to the front. When we went down the first big hill, Sable screamed so loud it hurt my ears. Then we rode the bumper cars and I ran her into the wall and she nearly bounced out of the car. After that we sat on the merry-go-round and talked about her problem, but not much. It was a day to have fun and leave all that other stuff back at home.

This morning I was really tired but I went to church anyway. Afterward, we went to Bob Evans for lunch. I didn't do much the rest of the day except study. I'm almost done with *The Odyssey*, but my favorite book is still *Lord of the Flies*. (I even like Piggy now.)

Dad and I are going to the baseball game again tomorrow. Dad said he would rather go to our games at school than to a Reds game. He thinks pro games cost way too much money nowadays. I think I'll call Allen to see if he wants to go with us. Kids aren't bothering him as much; he's even lost a few pounds. He said the other day if I could turn into a cool, skinny kid, then maybe he has a chance. I just laughed, because we both know that I'll never be a cool kid, no matter how much weight I lose. And you know, I don't even want to be one. Not if it means turning out like Nate.

Thursday, 4-26

Tonight I tutor Robb in math. Last week Mr. L told him that if he keeps working hard, he should have no problem passing Algebra I. And I think he's doing pretty good in his Algebra II class too. That would be great because he really has tried to do his best. Everyone has something they're good at, I suppose. Robb called yesterday to make sure we were still on for tonight. It makes me feel good to help him, but he doesn't want his buddies to know that he is getting help from a freshman. I can understand that.

This morning I saw a bluebird at the suet feeder Mom put in the backyard. It's been a long time since I've seen one. Probably sometime last fall, maybe even before we moved. When the light hit it just right, it was such a bright blue, it was like a piece of the sky flying around on earth. I called Mom to see it, but the bird flew away before she got there. I'll pay more attention and show her one this week.

It's almost time for Robb to come over so I need to eat dinner. Only five more Mondays to get up and then it will be summer. What a crazy school year!

Friday, 4-27

God really is testing me. Not as bad as He tested Job, but almost. What more can happen to my close friends? I feel like that guy on *Lost*—the big kid who won the lottery by using unlucky numbers. After he won, he brought bad luck to everyone associated with him. Guess you heard about Allen and how he fell over in PE class. I heard Coach Simmons made all the kids run around the gym for goofing off, and I guess it was too much for Allen. I didn't know that anything happened until lunchtime. Sable came running up to me and told me about how Coach performed CPR and then the ambulance came. We were afraid he died of a heart attack. I was glad when the principal came over the intercom and said Allen Zuekerman was doing better. His doctor said he would be just fine in a week or two.

Mom sent him a get-well card, and I'm going to visit him as soon as he can have visitors. Leave it to Allen to scare everybody half to death.

What's sick about the whole thing is that some kids still made fun of him. Acting like they were falling and putting their hands over their heart. I don't get what goes through some people's heads. When I told my mom about it, she said it's all about people judging others but never themselves. I watched a news show once where they were interviewing Mother Teresa. She said, "If we're too busy judging, then we don't have time to love," or something like that. She was really a cool lady. I mean nun. Whatever.

Tuesday, 5-1

Miracles of miracles. Spencer actually told me he was sorry. I was at my locker when he came up to me. "Hey, man. I'm really sorry about what happened."

I looked at him in disbelief and my first reaction was to punch him. But he did look really sorry, so I just shrugged and told him not to worry about it.

"Is he going to be okay?" Spencer asked.

"Who?"

"Allen. I heard he had a heart attack."

"Oh. Uh, yeah. He's gonna be fine. I went to see him Sunday."

"Glad he's hanging in there."

I turned back to my locker and didn't say anything else to him, so he left. I still don't get him. He pretended to be friends with me and Allen and even defended us. But in the end he betrayed us, especially me. It doesn't make any sense. I mean, how did setting me up make his life any different or any better? Maybe for a day he was sort of a hero and got a few laughs. But now he has to live with what he did. I certainly do. For a jerk like Nate, this wouldn't be a big deal, but Spencer's different. I think deep down he's really a nice guy—he just got caught up in what Robb calls the "jock mentality." Robb said his cousin played football at UT and the football team really did some awful things to this hooker who came to one of their parties. His cousin feels really ashamed of what he did. He says he'll have to live with it for the rest of his life and that he'll never get over it. Whenever he sees guys acting crude around a woman, he always tells them to knock it off. It's his way of trying to make up for what he did. This is how I bet Spencer feels. That's why he said he was sorry about Allen. He just can't apologize to me yet.

Thursday, 5-3

Seems weird to have both Sable and Allen back in school. Neither of them look any different, except Allen has lost a little weight. I'm probably the only one that noticed though. Poor Allen, he's on this strict diet, way worse than Weight

Watchers, and says he's starving most of the time. He said he'd kill for French fries; I told him they would kill him first. I was sorry as soon as I said it. But he just laughed and said he didn't want to go back to the hospital again. "Ever since I saw the movie *One Flew Over the Cuckoo's Nest*, I don't trust hospitals, especially nurses. They yell at me about eating too much. And some of them are bigger than me," Allen grumbled. That's what I don't get. There are more overweight adults than overweight kids, but it's us kids who get ridiculed the most. I guess it's because people think of kids as naturally skinny, and middle-aged adults as naturally fat. But fat is fat, no matter what age a person is. Bad is bad.

I forgot to mention the latest news about the second victim. She was another overweight teenage girl but a couple of years younger than Kimberly Taylor. She went to school at Westwood High, way on the other side of town. If Paul was around, I bet he would want us to go check it out. It really makes me wonder if the killer found out Paul was trying to catch him. Maybe losing weight is saving me in more ways than I know.

Sunday, 5-6

Please Don't Read This Page

I had my first real date this weekend. It was with Sable. It was kind of awkward at first, because she was the one who asked me out. She put a note in my locker, asking me out for coffee and dessert Saturday night. When I called her about it, she said her mom would drop us off and pick us up. When I told my mom about it, my sister overhead me. "Jimmy's going on a date!" she squealed and grabbed her heart.

"Yeah, and I won't be sneaking in at two in the morning."

"Shut up, Jimmy."

Mom just rolled her eyes.

My sister and Mom were acting so stupid about the whole thing, it seemed like forever before Sable and her mom picked me up. It felt funny with her mom driving and me and Sable sitting in the back. I kept trying to include Mrs. Moore in the conversation so she wouldn't think Sable and I were trying to make out or anything. But Sable didn't help matters any. She kept smiling at me and moving real close. It seemed like forever before we got to Starbucks. Her mom was real cool though, and when we got out of the car, she said, "Have a good time."

The last time I had been in Starbucks was the afternoon Paul and I hid in the restroom from my sister and her friends. I hadn't thought about that for months. That was a close call. I hate to think what my sister would have done had she seen us.

A sense of relief washed over me as we went inside.

"What do you usually drink?" Sable asked as we walked up to the counter.

"Water, usually."

"You need to try one of their coffee drinks. They are soooo good."

Sable knew what she wanted right away, and ordered a venti mocha with whipped cream. It took me longer to make up my mind because I don't really like coffee. I finally settled on a sugar-free vanilla latte with skim milk. The cheesecake in the case looked good, so I decided to splurge. I had watched my points all day so I had enough left to get dessert. Sable ordered a large piece of chocolate cake with raspberry sauce inside.

"Guess you're eating again," I said as I pulled out my wallet.

Sable frowned and shook her head. "I asked you, remember? My mom gave me some money. Besides, it's the least I can do for someone who practically saved my life."

Before I could say anything, the Starbucks guy put our drinks on the counter. "We'll bring your cake over to you," he said.

We found a table near the front of the store next to a guy reading a newspaper. Right outside the window a group of girls stood around smoking cigarettes. We could hear piped in guitar music. The place was full of teenagers, but I didn't see anyone I recognized.

"I think I'm getting better, Jimmy. Look." Sable rolled up her sleeves and there were no fresh scars.

"That's really cool. Bet your parents are happy."

"Yeah, they've been great. My therapist asked if she could talk with them about some things, so I finally gave her permission. She said they needed to know the truth about why I cut myself." Sable took a long drink of her mocha. "At first I didn't want them to know—I didn't want to cause trouble in the family, but Annie, my therapist, said there already was trouble in the family."

"I thought it was because of your brother—with his autism and everything."

"That was part of it. Annie said I was mad because my brother's problems were visible, but no one could see mine. And I wanted my parents to know that I was way more messed up than my brother."

The guy came with our desserts and left.

"Do you want me to tell you why?" Sable asked.

"It doesn't matter. You'd still be the same old Sable to me."

"Thanks, Jimmy," she said, looking relieved. "But I need to let you know that I'm not as freaky as I seem." She took another sip of her mocha and cleared her throat. "It was my grandfather. He was a real creep—he used to watch me when I was little. He died when I was seven. My mom cried when I told her about Pa Pa. She said she was so sorry; she should have paid more attention. There were always rumors about him. My grandmother divorced him when my mom was only five, so she never really knew him that much." She looked down at her coffee. "He seemed like a nice guy when they reconnected years later. Mom's older sister hated him, but never said why. Mom was thrilled that he liked me so much; she thought he was just a doting grandfather." Sable had tears in her eyes and I took her hand.

"It's not fair, Sable. It's not fair you had to go through all that. Your grandfather's the freak, not you. Oh my god, like in *Lord of the Flies*, your grandfather was the beast. I just don't get things. I don't get why people are mean. Why do adults hurt little, helpless kids? It's no wonder kids hurt each other. I mean, it's really bad when people are considered heroes for only doing what's right. Like that guy in the news they made a big deal out of because every year he gives poor kids money for school supplies. My dad does stuff like that all the time, and he would be embarrassed if the news people called him a hero."

Sable stared at me for a while. Then she said, "Do you want to go somewhere and make out?"

My neck instantly felt hot. Talk about changing the subject. I hope nobody heard her say that.

We didn't of course, because there was no place to go. And, I wouldn't have made out with her anyway, but I might have kissed her. We didn't talk about any more heavy stuff for the rest of the night. Just school, Sable's favorite Death Cab For Cutie CD, Allen, Robb, some of Sable's friends, and, of course, Paul.

But at least the air was cleared. And Sable knew she could trust me with her secret.

Monday, 5-7

I have some bad news about Paul. He's not dead but he did get injured really bad. Something about his legs, I guess he broke them. My dad found out at church. Paul's grandmother said that she is helping bring him home from Colorado and that Paul would need some friends to help him adjust. Dad isn't quite sure what happened. Maybe he just doesn't want to tell me yet. Paul's grandmother said he had mentioned knowing me from church and that's how she knew where to find me.

I thought I'd never hear from him again. When he left, nobody had a clue where he went. They had everybody looking—it was even on TV for a day. I guess he went to Colorado. Or at least ended up there.

The baseball game yesterday was exciting. We beat Brookview, which was great because we hate them. Everybody on our end of town does. They are such jerks and poor losers. Most of us think they did all the vandalism this past football season. If something else gets spray-painted, it's probably because we beat them again.

I have a math test tomorrow and I should go study but first I want to tell you this. The other day, Mr. L called the quadratic formula the aquatic formula just to be funny, but some students were half-paying attention. Today, when he asked Whitney what she could use to solve a problem, she said, "The aquatic formula!" It was pretty funny. Some kids never listen and then wonder why they don't do well on tests.

Thursday, 5-10

What an awful day this has been. During second period this morning someone squirted pepper spray in a class or maybe a bathroom. Whichever, it got in the ventilation and all of a sudden everyone was coughing and crying. Mr. Larson took us outside. It really burns and takes forever to go away. One student who has asthma had to go home or maybe to the doctor. I hope they find out who it was cause that stuff hurts. I couldn't imagine getting sprayed like those guys on the *Cops* show. That would make you mad enough to really do something wrong. But you can't see, so I guess it works. I had to take out my contacts and wash them in the water fountain. I couldn't stop rubbing my eyes. When I get home, I know Mom is going to ask what happened, like why I've been crying. I can see it now. She'll think someone said something mean to me, and then get on the phone asking Sable's mom if there really was pepper spray at school. I can't wait to say, "I told you so."

Mom worries that I still get picked on but I'm okay now. I mean, some people still bother me about stuff but I don't listen like I used to. It makes Nate and his "boys" mad when they don't see me get all flustered. In a way, I have them to thank for losing weight. If they had never made fun of me, I wouldn't have gotten fed up. That's funny, fed up. My folks want me to eat less but they also want me to be happy. And eating made me happy. Really happy. Those warm chocolate chip cookies in the cafeteria were in my dreams. But I can't go back to that. If I ever get big again, then I'll be the one running, I mean walking, away this time. Now that I have a routine and my dad works out with me, I enjoy my life. My sister actually told me she was proud of me, even though I think it about made her want to puke to say it. I'm not sure if Mom made her do it, but I think she was sincere. I guess I'll always be her little brother no matter now big I get, as in older.

Later this week, Paul is coming home. His granny told Dad that Paul would be in a hospital for a while, probably for tests and stuff, like when I go for my checkups. She said it would be great if me and some others could go visit. I'll ask Allen and Sable.

Friday, 5-11

Usually I would have put Please Don't Read This Page on this entry, but it's okay if you read it. I want you to know why I am so depressed in class. Dad told me last night what happened to Paul. When he was in Colorado, he and another runaway were trying to jump onto a train so they could go to LA. Paul got his arm caught and then he tripped and fell. His legs landed on the tracks and before he could pull them away, the wheels came along and cut them off. I think they were just dangling but the doctors amputated them at the hospital. That was two months ago and now he's coming home. I feel so bad for him and yet I'm scared to go see him. I've never been around someone with no legs, and I'm afraid I'll say something wrong or stare at where his legs used to be. He's at Children's

Hospital, so I'm getting checked out early. Dad said they would be fitting Paul with new legs. Prosthetics they're called. I had to look that word up in the dictionary and it took me forever to find it. All I can think of is the scene in *Forrest Gump* when Lt. Dan comes home with his new legs, and Forrest is talking about them in his funny voice. I will let you know how it goes at the hospital. Thanks for reading this, Mrs. Pope.

Saturday, 5-12

Today was difficult. More for me than Paul. He's had time to get used to the fact that he doesn't have legs, but it's going to take me awhile. I mean, he still regrets everything that happened but I think he's gotten counseling. Probably lots of it. He talked about his dad more than he ever did before. He told me that when his dad killed himself, he thought it was because he was a bad kid, but now Paul knows that depression was the reason. Somewhere, I think in health class, they told us that depression runs in families. I didn't mention it to Paul but I might one day. I bet his doctors have already figured that out.

My dad didn't stay in the room the whole time; he let me and Paul just talk. I think it was so I could learn how to deal with things. He had told me before we got to the hospital how important it is for me to treat Paul like he's normal old Paul, the normal that was good.

Funny thing, Paul didn't recognize me for a second. Even though he was just waking up, I know it was really because of the weight I lost. I mean, after the last eight pounds, I'm down to 137. That's like losing half a person.

I started to introduce myself as some other kid, but then Paul's eyes opened wide.

"Man, what happened? I almost didn't know who you were."

"I decided to lose some weight, sort of for survival," I said, smiling.

Paul laughed and said he had lost a little weight too. I felt a bit awkward and tried not to look down at the sheets where his legs should have been.

He asked all about school and everyone there. I told him Whitney was still the same "skanky ho." Paul said he never thought he would hear me say those words and laughed real loud. The kid in the bed next to Paul told him to shut up. He was in a wreck because he was driving drunk and now has all these tubes in him—he has a real bad attitude. His face's all bandaged up and he curses all the time. But at least he has his legs. Maybe that's mean of me to say. I mean, how would I feel if my face were covered up and I was in pain and stuff. Guess you never know how you'll react to things until you're dealing with them.

On the way home, I told Dad that I thought it was weird how Paul seems happier now than before he ran away. When he had both this legs, his life was miserable. His dad kills himself and Paul runs away and gets his legs cut off and now he acts like a normal kid. Life is mixed up sometimes. I can barely figure out my life, much less Paul's.

Sunday, 5-13

Happy Mother's Day, Mrs. Pope. I gave my mom a bottle of her favorite perfume, and Dad, Jessica and I have to fix dinner for her tonight. Mom said the best present is for us to let her lounge around all day and read romance novels.

After church, Dad dropped me off at the hospital, while he played nine holes of golf. This time I didn't dread going. Paul's attitude makes it easier. When I got there, I got off on the wrong floor. It must have been the cancer floor because there was this little bald-headed kid walking right in front of the elevator. He was rolling a metal thing that had a bag of clear liquid on it and a tube running to his arm. Right away, I knew this wasn't Paul's floor and I got back on the elevator. But in that few seconds, the little kid looked at me. He had dark circles under his eyes and he was real pale; I couldn't tell how old he was, maybe ten. Then he smiled and said, "Good morning, how are you?" I tried to answer but words wouldn't come out. I punched the button to close the doors, but he stood there and watched as the doors closed. Before they did, I said, "I'm okay. Have a good day." And then the doors shut. I think I will remember his eyes for a long time. It makes me sad.

Paul talked about his mother some. He said that after his father died, his mom finally admitted to her drinking problem. She was the last one to figure that out. He says that she might go to one of those AA meetings. I remember when I was young and heard Dad say he was going over to AAA to pick up something, like a map, and I thought he had a problem.

I told Paul all about the police coming to my house and what they said about the predator. He hadn't heard about the second murder, but smiled real wide when I told him he was right about the kid being innocent. "Maybe I should go into the FBI or CIA," he said. "Do you think I got the right guy? That would be really cool."

"He's one of the suspects, so you got that part right. But my dad said these things take years. Some murders are never solved."

"Just wait till I'm an FBI agent. I'll solve them all. *Cold Case* Paul, that's me."

"Glad you've decided to wait," I told him. "We've got more important things to investigate. Like getting through high school. And girls."

"Girls? Are you the Jimmy Winterpock I know?"

Before I could answer, the doctor came in and talked to Paul about fake legs. Stuff like how they work, how to put them on. Paul asked if I wanted to see what was left of his legs but I told him no. Maybe one day I will.

Me and Dad worked out when we got home from the hospital. After visiting Paul, I needed to burn some energy. I can be worried about something, like school, or Sable, or Spencer, or whatever, and once I get to straining and sweating on the weights, I forget about what's bugging me. Some things, like Nate, take a harder workout. And that little bald-headed kid's eyes.

Tuesday, 5-15

There was something I didn't want you to read about me and Paul. At the beginning of the school year, we tried to use MySpace to catch the killer of Kimberly Taylor. We put my sister's picture on the Internet to see if the killer would contact her (which meant us). I was so afraid she would find out it was Paul and me who did it. Back then, I thought if she knew it was me, I would've been the next murder victim. Anyway, tonight it all came up again. We were in the family room watching *Dancing with the Stars*, when the news interrupted some old guy doing the tango with this hot babe. They said it was breaking news—that the police had arrested someone for the two murders. It's some guy who was a former counselor at Kimberly's high school. Looks like all of us were wrong.

Anyway, we were all sitting there glued to the TV and after a while my sister said, "Mom, I wonder if the killer stalked Kimberly from her MySpace site?"

My ears lit up and my neck turned red.

"Maybe," Mom said. "But let's not bring that up again. It stills scares me to think someone did that to you, honey." Then Mom got all quiet and she squinted her eyes at Jessica. "I wonder if the killer was stalking you."

My sister opened her mouth and acted like she was about to cry. I was sitting there unable to speak, trying to act like I was watching the news. Then the phone rang and it was Paul. "Not now. Yes, I saw it. I'll call you back," I said.

I had to say something. "That's crazy. Her counselor? Guess the boyfriend is innocent." And I went back to eating my bowl of popcorn. Jessica was facing away from me, half-crying and half-snorting. Then my sister gave out this big wail like she had seen an alien or something.

"Who could have stalked me, Mom?" she whined. "We never found out. I could be dead."

All I could think was how I might be dead too.

"I don't know but when I talked to the police about it—"

(I'm thinking POLICE!) "—they said that if they can catch them, they might grow old in jail."

My popcorn started to taste real funny and the TV was just a blur. I think I sat there with my mouth hanging open, staring straight ahead, picturing me and Paul as roommates in the big-house. Itchy and Scratchy. Bevis and Butthead. Gimpy and Stimpy. Friends and cellmates forever.

Jessica was still crying a little and she asked Mom, "Who do you think would do that to me?"

My vision cleared up. "I don't know," Mom said. "An old boyfriend?"

"Maybe. But I think I know . . ."

My heart was about to jump out of my nose.

"I think it's—" and then she turned around real fast and pointed at me "—it's Jimmy!"

I spit chewed popcorn all over the TV.

Then my mom and my sister started laughing. And in between crying from laughing so hard, they told me that they knew a long time ago. It turned out that Danny saw us run into the bathroom. So, my sister stayed in Starbucks extra long so I would have to sit in the bathroom for two hours. And when the show was over, they were still laughing, and when I was lying in the bed, I could hear them laughing.

Hahaha. Everybody laughs at Jimmy. Yukk, yukk at Jimmy. I guess it is better than being killed by your sister.

I decided to keep their little joke from Paul, at least until he finishes high school. I wouldn't want to do anything to discourage him from being an FBI agent.

Sunday, 5-20

This week we have a big math test. That really bites for Mr. L to give us a big test right before finals. I've been helping Robb and I sure hope he does better. His dad is giving him grief about his grades and his scholarship. The last time I was over there, his dad was yelling at him, saying he wasn't going to pay for college if Robb failed math. Man, that's pressure. I'm lucky I don't have to worry about passing my classes. But I bet Robb never had to worry about making any team he tried out for, so I guess we're even. Robb said he feels bad for how he treated me in PE, but I told him not to worry about it. "There've been kids way worse than you."

"Yeah, like Nate. I should have shut that little piece of white trash up. I could have, you know. But I didn't think it bothered you that much." He gave me a sheepish half smile. "Sorry, about that, man. But next time? Just wait till he tries to pull that crap on you."

There aren't too many kids that will speak up for someone if they don't know them. Is that something people learn when they grow up? It seems to me that it's either there or it's not. I believe that I learned how to think of others in church. My preacher talks a lot about helping those in need. And my parents do too. Some kids I see in church don't act like they should—the preacher's sermons last about as long as the walk to their car in the church parking lot.

We had a sub in history and it took about ten minutes to do my worksheet. Since I had already read the chapter, it didn't take long. One kid asked if he could go to the bathroom and he didn't come back till the end of the period. Boy, did he reek. The teacher didn't say anything but we noticed. If you don't smoke, which I don't, it's easy to tell. I couldn't ever imagine kissing a girl who smokes. I bet it would be like licking an ashtray and I'd want to puke.

Now, I'm in homeroom with no HW to do.

I think I will ask Sable if she wants to go with me to visit Paul. I'm glad she doesn't smoke.

Monday, 5-28

Today's Memorial Day, but no one feels like doing much because of Paul. And then Robb called all scared he might not graduate. "If you're not doing anything, you want to come over? I worked the problems you gave me, and I think I did them right. But I need you to watch me do them a few more times." Dad dropped me off, and Robb's dad was supposed to take me home but my dad called and said he would pick me up. He said he thought we should visit Paul. I asked Robb if he wanted to go with us and meet Paul. He said he would, so I decided to use the time in the car to drill him on more problems.

When we got there, Robb went right up to Paul and shook his hand. "Hey, man, glad to meet you. Jimmy says you're really cool." At first Paul acted like he didn't want Robb there but then he was okay with it. I sure wasn't going to tell Robb that he couldn't come in, so I'm glad it worked out. We wheeled Paul around the floor and talked about school and parents and the hot girls in school. Some of them on our lists matched but a lot didn't. When Robb said he thought Sable was cute, Paul looked at me and then told Robb that she was someone I liked. Robb slapped me on the shoulder and called me a "love god." Paul thought that was so funny. Ha-ha.

Robb told Paul how sorry he was about everything and how he had a friend in elementary school who ran away, but his parents found him hiding in the barn out back of their neighbor's house. The dog kept barking and gave him away. When the dog started sniffing around the shed, it scared a rat that was living in there. The rat ran out right across the kid's foot and then he screamed and knocked cans all over. It was pretty funny and we were all laughing. Then Robb admitted he was that kid. I think Robb will go back to the hospital with me. He has a car too.

Tuesday, 5-29

I forgot to talk about Paul's new legs in my last entry. It'll take at least six months or more for his stumps to heal, then he can get fitted for fake legs. Paul showed us some pamphlets on artificial legs and they look really cool. Totally bionic. Man, he's going to look like C-3PO from *Star Wars*. He showed me pictures of the silicone liners that go on first, then these legs made out of carbon. And there's this really awesome tube that makes the foot move. There's all these smaller components in between and the knee joint looks like something from *Terminator 3*. From what I overheard my dad and Paul's grandmother talking about, Children's Hospital is helping pay for them so he can get the good ones. He has to go through months of physical therapy, but at least he'll be able to walk again and not have to sit in a wheelchair forever. And he'll have some really cool legs, like Lieutenant Dan in *Forrest Gump*. When he gets his new legs, I'll say, "Lieutenant Paul, you've got magic legs."

Paul said at first he didn't want to live when he woke up

and realized his legs were gone. But now he feels okay about things. His doctor told him about a website and chat room for amputees called Amplife.org, and that's been a big help. He said it's unbelievable what some of the amputees can do. They play all kinds of sports and some have even qualified for the Boston Marathon. I told Paul I wouldn't have known about all these cool things if it weren't for him. When he gets a little better, his doctor suggested he go to an in-hospital therapy group for amputees. Paul asked me if I would go to the first meeting with him. He said he might need some support, since he didn't get his legs blown off because of a war or anything, and the people there might think he's really stupid for jumping trains. I told him I'd go with him, but that no one would think he was a stupid kid. They would think he was one mixed-up, brave kid. Paul smiled when I said that.

I wanted to tell him that he thinks he's stupid because he has all of his dad's mean words still stuck inside him somewhere. But I didn't say anything, because it's too soon to disrespect the dead.

Wednesday, 5-30

I couldn't wait to get home and write this entry. Today might have been one of the best of my life. I KISSED SABLE!! Yay for Jimmy Winterpock! Actually, Sable cornered me on the stairs and kissed me but it still counts. We were going down the back stairwell at church (yes, church) when she stopped in front of me and turned around. I said, "What?" but I sort of knew "what." Sable stepped up one step and put her arms around me. "Kiss me, Jimmy. Hurry, before someone opens the door." And I just reacted like I'd been waiting for her to ask or something. I mean, it was great. I think I had my eyes open but I didn't on the second one. Yes! Two! Then we hustled down the stairs and into the lobby near the youth room. Jeff, our youth minister, was standing there. He looked at me real funny. "Winterpock" was all he said, but it sounded like he was asking if I had been smooching with Sable. Then, if that wasn't bad enough, our preacher went on and on about temptation. I think he must have seen us—I couldn't even look at him during his sermon. I mean, geesh, can't they leave a "love god" alone?

But you know what, kissing a girl is a natural thing. Where do you think all the people in church come from? As far as I know, there is only one virgin birth. What I'm saying is, all I did was kiss Sable. And it was nice. I can't wait to do it again. But this time, I'll go first. Could this mean that I, Not-So-Slim-Jimmy, has a girlfriend? Like Mr. L says, "I guess the planets are aligned."

Thursday, 5-31

In science, I saw someone I used to think was pretty copying answers from the kid's test next to her. You can probably figure out who, I mean "whom," and I don't care if she gets in trouble. My teacher can be clueless sometimes about cheating. Students will do it right in front of the teacher and not get caught. No one cheats much in English, especially if we're writing essays. But it makes me mad when they do it in science and math, because I study for hours and then they come along and get an A without doing anything. When they get a good grade, they wave it around like they did it themselves, but everyone knows they copied. It really burns me when the teacher tells them how smart they are or if I hear them bragging about their GPA.

After class, in the hall, I told Whitney that she didn't need to cheat, she's just as smart as anybody in there. The girl next to her overheard me and said, "Who cares? As long as she gets a good grade." Whitney giggled at me and said just because I lost weight, it didn't make me all that special. I started to say I didn't mean it that way but she said, "You know what, Jimmy, you'll always be the fat kid who tried to make out with me at the party." She had to know how much that hurt, and I tried not to let her see it but I think she did. I just went on to class. When Allen tried to talk to me, I didn't have a lot to say.

I went to see Paul tonight. Sable and Robb went with me. We rolled Paul around the floor, just talking about school and things. Robb told us he is doing better in math and should get his scholarship to Bowling Green. That would be so cool to know someone playing college football. He said we should all come to a game. The school is somewhere in Ohio so that's not too far away. I know Dad would take us for the weekend. He enjoys ball games.

Next year, I'm going to some of our football games, now that I have Sable to sit with. Maybe Dad will go too. He used to play in high school; I think it was on the line, maybe a tackle.

You will not believe what happened at the hospital. I can't believe I forgot to tell you this first. We were pushing Paul up and down the halls and we ended up in the waiting area and one of the funniest, scariest things I have ever seen happened. An old lady was sitting in there, and there was a bunch of kids also. A big table was in front of her. When we walked by, she looked up and then kind of leaned forward and jumped at us, but she had her hand over her eye. Next, I heard a thud on the table and the lady yelped like a dog and started reaching for this ball rolling across the table. The ball was her eye! It had fallen right out of her head. And the kids sitting there started screaming and this old lady was bent over, chasing her eye across the floor. We all froze and then Sable yelled, which made me jump out of my shoes. Finally, the old lady stopped it with her foot and took it over to the water fountain and washed it off. Then she pushed it back in and just went back and sat down. It all happened real fast. Paul laughed so hard I thought we were going to have to call a doctor. It was pretty funny. I am surprised some of those little kids sitting there didn't have a heart attack.

Saturday, 5-2

Sable is much better. I think she's finally listening to her counselors.

I wasn't in your class yesterday, because I had to go to the doctor. The visit turned out to be pretty good. The nurse put me in this room and I waited forever. I got cold in there. Finally, Dr. Weber came in the door, examining my chart. He looked up and instead of saying anything, he checked the name on the folder. "Jimmy Winterpock?"

That made me feel good and I said, "Yep, it's really me. Or what's left of me."

"It says here you were sixty pounds heavier in November. What happened to you?"

I told him how I started running and working out with my dad.

"Working out?" Dr. Weber stared at me for a minute. Then he said, "Jimmy, is there something wrong?"

I said no, nothing is wrong. But he didn't believe me, because he called my dad in from the waiting room. Dad told him the whole story, or most of it.

Then the doctor checked my heart and listened to my lungs and poked my knee and all the other things they do.

Before we left, he told me I was in great health. Well, maybe not great but so much better than I had been. "Why? How?" he asked. I told him it was because he said I would be fat forever. And then I told him some of the things kids said to me. And how much it hurt and how they treated Allen. I said I didn't want to be Not-So-Slim-Jimmy forever and that I wanted to go to a football game and not be laughed at. And how I didn't want to die young. And a lot of other things that happened this year.

I think Dr. Weber had tears in his eyes, and so did my dad. Then Dr. Weber put his hand on my shoulder and said he didn't know many adults who had as much discipline as I had. He said if I could do this, I could do anything in life. "You must have gone through a lot," he said.

I laughed at that and said, "You have no idea."

I guess I should be proud of all the weight I lost, but it seems easy now that I look back. It's hard to understand how I could have ever been the kid who ate all the time. But it was me. I could tell that by all the clothes I gave to Goodwill. Even my shoe size is different. When I ask Mom about all the money she had to spend on new stuff for me, she says she's not sure if it was worth it. Then she laughs and smiles. My sister is different, a little. She still finds other things to complain about, thinking it's her job to point out any cracks in my armor. Dad is real proud of me. All the working out we did helped him too. I guess we all got better in some way.

Monday, 5-4

Math class was super today. Nate must have decided that since the year is almost over, he's running out of "pick-on-Jimmy" time. Mr. L was up at the board working another problem in his most boring voice, when a paper ball hit me in the head. I looked over at Nate and he was smiling. I picked up the paper and opened it. "I miss your boobs!" was written on it. And of course, that's when Mr. L decided to notice me. He asked me what I was doing. I didn't feel like covering for Nate anymore, so I said I was reading a note that Nate had thrown at me. Mr. L looked over at Nate and gave him a mean look. Nate got all upset and said, "Jimmy is lying, the big fat loser."

Mr. L started to write on the board, then changed his mind and put down the marker. He turned around and walked over to Nate's desk. Everyone got real quiet, even Nate. Mr. L said, "I think not. I believe that you, Nate, are the biggest loser." Everyone in class started clapping. Nate sputtered for everyone to stop. Then he told the class to "piss-off." Mr. L walked over to the intercom button and pushed it. When the office responded, Mr. L said he had an unruly student who needed to be removed. In a minute or two, an officer (I still don't know his name) came down and took Nate away. Wow! What a day! I just hope I don't get pounded on by Nate tomorrow. But, you know, it probably would be worth it.

Study, study, study. That's all I've been doing. The only break I have is helping Robb study for his math final. The pressure should be off of him, since he already has a high enough grade to pass even if he chokes, but Robb says he wants to do well on the final for the principle of it. And to wave it in his father's face. "Maybe that will shut him up once and for all. I'm tired of him calling me an idiot." His dad's always nice to me whenever I go over there—I guess he thinks I'm Robb's savior or something. Robb gets down about how his dad treats him though. He says his dad's nice to everyone but him. I think his dad worries that Robb might get mixed up with the wrong crowd or get his girlfriend pregnant, so he figures if he's hard on him about the little things, Robb will be too scared to do something really bogus (like getting a DUI or trashing his hotel). Some parents think that being overly strict makes kids turn out to be model citizens. But some psychologist I saw on *Dateline* said that kids raised with strict discipline don't turn out any better than kids who come from permissive homes. Kids just need to know that they have parents, or at least someone, willing to put them at the top of their list.

Tuesday, 6-5

What a year. I remember complaining about having to write in a journal and now I can't wait to write down what happened. Finals start tomorrow but these are due Friday, the last day of school. I want you to know that you are one of the best teachers I've ever had, and my journal really helped me make it through some tough times this year. I wish I had been writing before now, but maybe this year I was ready for something like this. Writing my thoughts on paper has made it easier for me to say things to people. Like how much I appreciate what I have and how much I love my parents and even my sister.

I'm sorry I didn't trust you in the beginning, but hey, I was a freshman who didn't know any better. If you want to read any of my other entries, that's okay. One day, I might show this to my kids, so don't throw it away, I'd like to get it back. They might get a charge out of knowing their dad was a big fat kid. And who knows, it might help them get through some things. I remember my grandfather talking about his childhood, but I was too little to really understand half of what he was saying. I wish now he had kept a journal. I bet some of what he was trying to tell me would make sense now.

Anyway, thanks, Mrs. Pope, for "freeing my muse," and "oiling my inner tin man."

Friday, 5-8

We turn in our journals today—right after our final—and it makes me sad. I will keep writing if you want to see what I do over the summer.

Sable, Robb and me are taking Paul to see the Reds play on Friday. His doctor made arrangements for us to meet some of the players. His doctor's good friends with Johnny Bench, one of those old players from the seventies. Anyway, Mr. Bench is in the Hall of Fame for being an awesome catcher, and he came and visited Paul last week. Actually, he visited a lot of kids, which is great. I think Paul made a good impression on him, and that's why Mr. Bench gave Paul free tickets to the game. We have seats right behind home plate and get to wheel Paul through the VIP entrance so he doesn't have to fight the stairs or the crowds. Paul's pretty excited about the whole thing.

Before I go up to see Paul, there's something I have to do.

There's a little bald-headed kid on the third floor I need to say "hey" to. I want to tell him to hang in there, because the world's a pretty good place, after all.

Thanks for everything.

Your student,

Jimmy Winterpock

Afterword

by Doug Hennig

Middle school was hard for me. I moved to a new town the summer before school started, so I didn't have any friends. I hoped to make some friends during the first few weeks of school, but no one gave me a chance. It was the same thing everyday. As I walked down the hallways, snickers and weird looks (or no looks at all) always followed me. I knew that I was overweight, but I grew up in a strong Christian family who believed that outward appearance doesn't matter. Inward beauty should be the focus of our lives. But inward beauty meant very little to the kids at my middle school. Outward appearance meant everything, especially if you were cool. For those of us who didn't quite fit the mold, life became a nightmare.

The first day came with many papers that my parents had to sign, confusion about which room to go to, and what to get for lunch – and with all this going on, not one person talked to me. Okay, it was only the first day, I thought. Everyone was busy and confused, maybe tomorrow. Then tomorrow came but still no one talked to me. Days and weeks passed and nothing changed. I kept to myself, doing my school work, while others talked to their friends and laughed. Everyday I would go to lunch, get my tray of food and then stand there, looking for somewhere to sit. As I stood there with my usual soft tacos, Doritos, and blue-raspberry All-Sport, I looked at a room with kids running everywhere. Kids eating, talking, laughing, running, pushing to get a better seat. An entire roomful of kids everywhere and

I felt so alone. How could someone feel so alone with so many people surrounding them? I would wander around until I found a table with no one else sitting at it, bless my lunch, and begin to eat my food, keeping my eyes down, staring at my food.

One day, on my way to my saxophone lesson, my mom asked me how I was doing. Immediately my eyes started to tear up. How could my mom know what I was going through? I began to cry and told my mom that I wasn't meeting anyone (but left out the part about being teased). I cried the entire way to my lesson and later that night. The entire time, I had been praying to God that He would help me. That He would put a friend in my life. But more than that, I asked him to give me the strength to get through each day. And He did. But there were still many nights where I would stay awake wondering why we had to move; wondering if there was a way for me to go back; wondering if things were ever going to change.

My family decided a few months later that we should try visiting some churches closer to us, so that my sister and I could make some friends in the youth group that would also go to school with us. After a few times in the Sunday school classroom and going on a weekend conference with the youth group, I was actually starting to meet some other people. And, I met a person my age who went to my school: Adam. Now I finally had someone to sit with at lunch! I was so excited! Adam introduced me to another one of his friends, Billy, who also went to the youth group. So I finally had a few friends to talk to. While that felt good, that didn't hide the fact that I was still getting teased every day.

Gym class was the worst. Kids would say some really mean things; it seemed like the cruelty would never stop. "What are you doing in the guys locker room?" kids would ask. "Shouldn't you be in the women's locker room?" "How did you get so big?" "Do you eat McDonalds every day?" They'd laugh for a while, and then start up again. "Watch out, porker coming through." Every single day. And they thought they were so funny. And I just took their insults and never said anything. I would just stare at the floor and pretend I didn't hear it . . . pretend that I didn't mind it . . . pretend it didn't hurt me. But every day, it wore on me and broke my heart again and again . . .

April 8th is my birthday and at that time every year I have a check up. I usually get to miss school because of it, but this year I wasn't so lucky and had to go after school. Like always, I sat in the waiting room until the nurse announced my name.

"Doug Hennig," she finally called. I followed her down the hallway and into one of the rooms. I jumped up on the high table with the plastic sheet that always crinkles when I sit on it. The nurse checked my blood pressure, height and, of course, my weight. The doctor came in and asked me how I was feeling and how school was going. I told him everything was okay. Then my doctor got a serious look on his face. He told me that he was concerned about my weight for someone my age. He showed me the chart for age, weight and height, and I was way above average for weight. And then he said something that changed my life: "Doug, if you don't deal with this problem now, you will have it for the rest of your life."

For the rest of my life? I thought. I expected this to last through middle school, and maybe high school, but for the rest of my life? Every day getting teased, ignored, and ridiculed? *Every day for the rest of my life?* This seemed to whirl around my head like a hurricane as my doctor kept talking about how bad it is for you to be overweight and what I should do. *If you don't deal with this problem now, you will have it for the rest of your life.* I kept repeating it in my head all the way home.

I went up to my room and lay on my bed, staring at the ceiling. *For the rest of my life. I can barely get through it right now. I can't go on like this the rest of my life. My weight is holding me back from so much that I could be doing.* And it was right then, in that moment, I realized what I had to do. I realized that I had to deal with this problem because I knew that I was not going to be able to live every day like this. And I knew God had bigger plans for me.

My family had a Total Gym exercise machine, and I asked my dad if I could work out with him. He was more than happy for me to exercise with him and it soon became a daily ritual for us. My dad taught me the exercises and we encouraged each other to keep going. Along with working out with my dad, I asked my mom if I could borrow her Weight Watchers books. The books assign points to food servings and gives you an allotment of points per day. I was allowed 26. So the summer began with daily workouts and food points.

Working out with my dad kept me focused. However, it was hard because I was not very strong. I always had to lower my weight amount. But it was a motivation so that I could be as strong as my dad. Some days I would feel so lazy and would not want to do anything. It would be raining and nasty outside and I would just want to sit back and watch television. *What is the big deal about missing a day? I'll just do it tomorrow.* But every single time I thought about working out, I would always think: *Do I really want this the rest of my life?* And that would be my focus.

And then there was the food. I love food. The year before, I would always come home and have a snack so that I could get my mind off school and just relax and have something to eat. I would always go back to seconds because my mom was such a great cook and because it made me feel good. However, now that I was on a diet, I couldn't use food for emotional comfort. It was hard when I was bored and at home because the refrigerator and pantry were so close. *What will a bag of chips hurt?* But then I would think about the kids who made fun of me.

I wanted to show those kids that I was more than someone who likes food – that I was more than a punching bag for them to make fun of – that I was a person just like them, with feelings and emotions.. Every single time I wanted to stop working out, I remembered how I was always the last one running at baseball practice, how I was put on the "skins" team at a soccer scrimmage, how I wasn't able to do any pull-ups or push ups in gym class and the jokes that came after it. *For the rest of my life? No.* Every single time I wanted to eat more, I remembered the jokes in the locker room about how big I was, the fingers pointed at me in the hallways, and the faces of the people who teased me and tried to ignore me. *For the rest of my life? No.* But more than anything, every single time I felt like I couldn't make it, I remembered how God had given me the strength to get through school and remembered that God had a bigger plan for me – that I was meant for something more than being made fun of – and that no matter what, He loved me for who I was.

The crude remarks and actions of my classmates helped keep me motivated, focused, and determined. And every single time I remembered just one joke that was made about me, it caused me to do an extra rep while working out or throw away another bag of chips. I knew that I could do something to change, and I was doing it. I was not going to live this way for the rest of my life. No. I did not have to take the words of others and let them tear me down. But I could take the words of others and let them change me for the better.

And the few friends that I did have helped encourage me and helped me get through the hard times. By spending time with them, I was able to see that they didn't care what I looked like – they liked me for who I was and it made me feel so great. By having the good times of sleepovers and days at the golf course, I was able to feel content about who I was. I was able to take my confidence and use it to keep on working out and dieting, knowing that I was doing this not to show off to other people, but for me.

At first, there was not a significant result from my working out and dieting. I lost a few pounds every week, but nothing too big. But I knew I had to keep with it. I was *not* going to live like this for the rest of my life. So I kept with it. And week by week, I lost a few pounds. Nothing big, nothing extreme. But I stuck with it. And slowly, slowly, I started to change. By the end of the summer, I was ready.

On the first day of high school, my sophomore year, I walked confidently into the building 45 pounds lighter. Walking through the hallways, I saw a sight that I had never seen before: people walking by me and making eye contact. People actually started talking to me in the classroom and I began making more friends. It was amazing. Nothing had ever changed about my personality, but people were willing to talk to me and have an actual conversation with me. And finally I felt something that I had never felt all my life: acceptance.

That year, I continued working out, waking up at 5 in the morning, and dieting. I lost another 10 pounds that year, making my weight loss a total of 55 pounds. I felt like a whole new person. I was able to make friends and even made the soccer team.

I went from being a kid who sat alone at the lunch table to being a cool kid people wanted to know. Who knew that 55 pounds could make such a difference? But why did it make such a difference? Because most people don't want to be friends with someone who is fat. That may seem bold to say, but I've been there and that seems about the best way to put it.

Kids spend too much time judging people by their looks. I don't know if it will ever change, but maybe my story will help at least one kid catch a break. Think about it. No one wants to be fat, no one wants to be an outcast, no one wants to be lonely. People just want to be accepted and understood. So when you see that kid sitting alone at the lunch table, maybe you'll understand him better and ask him something about himself. Maybe you'll make eye contact with the kid who can't afford to dress like everyone else, or smile at the kid who is too shy to smile first. You never know, it just might change *your* life.

Sincerely,

Doug Hennig

Acknowledgments

The authors of *The Fat Boy Chronicles* are deeply grateful to our friends and family who offered invaluable critical reaction to this novel in its many stages, and we are humbled by the generosity of their collective response.

Brad Baker and Morgan Eurek filtered Jimmy's world for teen authenticity, while George Weinstein, Mark All and Kathleen Boehmig provided support from the Four Elements.

Chattahoochee High's students and staff offered their heartfelt confidence in our work, and Northview High School offered the use of its hallway for the cover.

We are exceedingly grateful to Dr. Thomas Inge for his honest and meaningful Foreword. His devotion to solve the teen obesity problem is vital to the future of America.

And, we are honored to have Doug Hennig as our inspiration. Without him, Jimmy Winterpock and his journal would not exist. Doug's ability to lose excess pounds against insurmountable odds offers hope to all those who struggle with their weight.

We feel gratitude beyond what we can articulate to Bonnie and David Buchanan, Michael Buchanan's adventuresome and awesome parents; and to Don Lang, Diane Lang's life partner, and Diane's children, Amy and Donnie Lang, and Sarah and Chris Bollman, who helped make her writing life possible.

Finally, we are indebted to Keith Washington and Jason Winn for their loyalty, their patient trust, and their passionate response to our work.

Authors Diane Lang and Michael Buchanan have used their experience as high school teachers to write **The Fat Boy Chronicles**. Named *Teachers of the Year,* nominated for *Disney Teacher Awards*, and featured in USA Today for creativity in the classroom, their ability to communicate to students is evident. Other works by Lang Buchanan include the novel **Micah's Child** and screenplay **Treasure of the Four Lions.**

What others are saying about *The Fat Boy Chronicles.*

The Fat Boy Chronicles is a story told with humor and true insight into the world of an overweight adolescent. It reminds the reader of the real pains and joys of teenage life. Jimmy's honest, straightforward journal entries make for a revealing, yet entertaining read. He is an amazing hero.
~ Melinda Long, New York Times #1 Bestselling author of
How I Became a Pirate and *Pirates Don't Change Diapers*

It's rare a voice comes along in literature that speaks to teenagers in their own words. Lang Buchanan does just that with uncanny precision, taking us on a rollercoaster ride of the ups and downs, trials and tribulations, inner thoughts and insecurities to which the teen in all of us can relate.
~Michael Lucker~ Screenwriter of *Spirit, Home on the Range, Mulan II, Emperor's New Groove II, Lilo & Stich II, 101 Dalmations II*

Many teenagers experience painful personal dramas during their time in high school with periods of confusion and self-doubt. For overweight kids like "Jimmy," these challenges are added on top of the discrimination that he faces based only on what he looks like and not on who he is. How great that Jimmy can find his own strength from the inside out!
~Beth Passehl, MS, CPT, RYA
Family Wellness Coach

I laughed aloud by page 3 and had tears streaming down my face not too many pages after. Jimmy Winterpock could have been one of the many hundreds of young people I listened to over the years as a school counselor. *The Fat Boy Chronicles* should be in the hands of every educator, parent, and middle and high school student across this nation. Lang Buchanan-- the author of *Micah's Child*-- hit home with this remarkable work.
~Jo Ann G. Swafford, Ed. S.
Retired Teacher and Two-time Counselor of the Year

A great story. What's on the inside is important. It's a great book for health classes across America. Jimmy is on the bandwagon to fight obesity and for others to see the real person he is.
~Stephanye I. Peek *President-Elect* Georgia Association for
Health, Physical Education, Recreation, and Dance

Jimmy Winterpock is every teenager. Every adolescent has felt like Jimmy at some point during this tumultuous time. The difference is that Jimmy has one of the worst stigmata of adolescence—being extremely overweight. He faces ridicule and humiliation by his peers, and ignorance and apathy from his teachers.

But Jimmy did a remarkable thing. With a nudge from his doctor and the support of family and friends, he found the courage to change his life. And soon after, he began to lose weight. Not through temporary diets but with slow persistence, good nutrition and exercise. In other words, his new lifestyle helped him achieve his goal. Jimmy is an inspiration to anyone who wants to make a positive change in his or her life.

~Mark Wulkan, MD, *Associate Professor of Surgery and Pediatrics, Emory University, Children's Healthcare of Atlanta*

The Fat Boy Chronicles rings true from the first paragraph to the last. Jimmy Winterpock--your hilarious and hurting teenage hero--gets your attention immediately with his sharp sense of humor and guarded vulnerability. Lang Buchanan's instincts as teachers and writers make Jimmy's journal, and his journey, pitch perfect.

~ George Weinstein, author of *Jake and the Tiger Flight*

The Fat Boys Chronicles is a dynamic book. Jimmy Winterpock's story inspires all of us to openly talk with our children about health concerns. This novel is a must for high school teachers and students.

~Randee Nagler, Area Superintendent Fulton County School System

In *The Fat Boy Chronicles*, Lang Buchanan takes the reader vividly into the day-to-day life of an extremely obese teenager who chooses to fight back against the all-too-common abuse, defeat, sadness, neglect, and ridicule facing kids with a weight problem. The extraordinary aspect of this story is how we (and the teen) arrive at a certain peaceful calm after a raging battle. Set in Cincinnati, Ohio, the authors demonstrate the magnitude and power of the social stigmatism, isolation, peer confrontation, and inner conflict experienced by millions of American teens of today who are just like Jimmy Winterpock.

~Thomas H. Inge, MD, PhD
*Director of the Comprehensive Weight Management Program
Director of the Teen Longitude Assessment of Bariatric Surgery
Associate Professor
University of Cincinnati College of Medicine
Cincinnati Children's Hospital Medical Center*
www.cincinnatichildrens.org/weight